DEALERS' CHOICE

SUSAN HAYES

Copyright © 2020 Susan Hayes

Dealers' Choice

First Print Publication: July 2020

Cover Design: Mina Carter

Editor: Dayna Hart

Published by: Black Scroll Publications Ltd.

ISBN: 978-1-988446-67-7

DEDICATION

For my Mum and Dad, for all their love and support.

New game. New rules. One choice.

One bad decision plunged cyborg batch-brothers Victor and Ward into a nightmare they barely survived. Now, they're reclaiming their lives and trying to move forward, but it's a battle they can't win alone. Helping them let go of the past is a beautiful doctor with a soft heart and hard rules about never getting involved with her patients.

Dr. Xori Virness is everything an unmated Pheran female isn't supposed to be - independent, determined, and light years away from her home and family. Her life was just the way she wanted it. Then, two dark and dangerous men with battle-scarred psyches flew into her orbit, laying waste to her plans and tempting her to break her own rules.

When old enemies return with a new target, the brothers will have to make a choice. Surrender to the past, or fight for their future.

PROLOGUE

OUT ON THE edge of civilized space is a rag-tag collection of space stations and platforms known as the Drift. It's a haven for the hunted, the lost, and those seeking second chances. The people who live there hail from every species, class, and corner of the galaxy, but they all have one thing in common: they don't belong anywhere else.

There's nothing beyond the Drift but wild space and an asteroid belt full of ore-rich rocks. The asteroids are mined by hundreds of vessels and their hard-working crews. When the ships deliver their haul to be processed, those crews hit the infamous bars, casinos, and pleasure houses that are the Drift's primary source of income…and only source of entertainment.

It's a world of its own. One where corporations rule, the laws are flexible, and everything is for sale, for the right price.

Welcome to the Drift.

CHAPTER ONE

VIC POUNDED on the door to the sanitation cubby, barely managing to dial back his frustration enough to avoid denting the surface. "Move your lazy ass, or we're going to be late."

"Cool your boosters, we won't be late," Ward hollered over the sound of the water. "We're two minutes away."

"And we are supposed to be there in four minutes. Are your onboard systems malfunctioning or did you forget how to tell time?"

There was a muttered grumbling, but the shower shut off, and Vic breathed a quiet sigh of relief. He never knew what resistance he'd meet getting Ward to these sessions. His batch-brother's moods were harder to predict than a solar storm. Which was one of the reasons they *needed* to talk with Dr. Virness. She was their best chance at reclaiming some kind of normal life.

Though *normal* was probably too strong a word. They were cyborgs, built as disposable soldiers for a war their corporate masters claimed was bloodless.

The *fraxx* it was. The cyborgs had bled and died for them, and when the fighting was over, the corporations had tried to decommission their toys…only to discover that their creations were self-aware and violently opposed to being terminated.

There were only four of them left by then. His twin, Ward, and their batch-brothers, Toro and Jaeger. The rest of their batch-siblings were slaughtered in the wars. Four had become two after they were freed— Jaeger and Toro had chosen to go their own way. He couldn't blame his brothers for wanting to explore the galaxy on their own. Obedience was hard-coded into their programming, and he had been their leader since the moment they'd stepped out of their maturation vats.

Ward rushed into the main room of their shared quarters, his wet hair slicked back and his clothes clinging to his still-damp skin. "Alright, I'm ready. Happy?"

"Not yet. That will happen when I get to look at Dr. Virness' lovely face instead of your grumpy one."

Ward grunted. "We have the exact same face."

"And yet, somehow, I'm the pretty one."

"In your dreams. See, this is why we have to keep seeing the lovely little blue doctor. You're *fraxxing* delusional."

"Aha! You finally admitted it. You like her, too." They set off, still talking as they navigated the labyrinth of almost identical corridors that connected the Nova Club's staff area to the public areas. One of the perks to working for the club was the fact it came with affordable housing.

"Well, yeah. We're basically the same person. Same tastes, same looks. And yet somehow, I got all the charm."

Vic stayed quiet, savoring the win. Ward had always denied he had any interest in the Pheran doctor. Xori Virness was helping them heal the wounds that their nanotech and accelerated healing ability couldn't touch. She was treating the damage done to their psyches after they'd been taken prisoner, reprogrammed, and forced to work as killers for a shady group known as the Gray Men.

They were almost to the sim-pod area when Ward turned and glowered at him. "Just because you didn't say it doesn't mean I don't know what you're thinking. Yes, I like her. She's attractive, smart, and the gentlest being for light years. We're assassins, for *fraxx* sake. Do you really think she'd want to be with us?"

"I have to hope so, because I'd like to be with her as more than just patient and therapist. And for the record, we're *former* assassins, and we never had a choice."

"There's still blood on our hands, Fox. We're drenched in it. Nothing we do is going to make that go away."

"I don't believe that. We deserve to have a little good in our lives, Wolf." Since being freed, they often used the nicknames they'd chosen for themselves instead of the names assigned to them by their former owners.

Ward gave him a half-smile and clapped him on the shoulder. "I think *you* deserve that." He walked away before Vic could say anything. Not that he needed to. They'd had this conversation more than once, and so far, nothing had changed Ward's mind. He hadn't forgiven himself for the things he'd done while under the Gray's control. Vic was almost ready to move on with his life. Ward wasn't.

They reached the sim-pod section just as Xori and another of her patients, Tianna Astor, were saying goodbye, and he couldn't help but note that the newly-minted head of Astek Corp looked tired and a little unsettled. He extended his senses slightly, confirming that her pulse was elevated, and she was manifesting signs of emotional distress. He caught the last bit of Tianna's conversation, too.

"...harder than I thought it would be, but I'm glad I did it."

"You did very well." Xori's soft words made his heart do a double beat.

Veth, he loved the sound of her voice. Hell, he liked everything about her. From the delicate tufts on the tips of her pointed ears to the way her blue-striped skin darkened when she laughed. Today she was wearing a simple blue top that left her arms bare, and a long, flowing skirt that fluttered slightly in the downdraft from an overhead vent.

Beside him, Ward exhaled with a barely audible

whistle of appreciation. "She wore her hair down. Dammit, that's not playing fair."

One of his brother's favorite ways to avoid answering the doctor's questions was to try to change the subject. His preferred topic of late had been to ask Xori why she always wore her hair tied back. It had become something of an obsession.

Vic laughed. "Check and mate, Wolf."

"Smug is not a good look for you." Ward's gaze was locked on Xori.

He couldn't blame him. With her hair loose, the doctor looked softer somehow, the waves of blue falling past her shoulders in a silken tumble he itched to touch.

Xori turned toward them, smiling in greeting. "You're right on time."

Tianna grinned. "Since your next victims are here, I'll get out of your way. There's a large slice of cherry pie waiting for me upstairs."

Tianna shifted to the internal comms channel all the cyborgs at the Nova Club shared. *"It's not easy, but I think she's onto something. Good luck."*

"You too. The last time I saw your husbands they were headed for the gaming tables with a stack of chips and no supervision."

"V'eth! That's my money they're playing with. The least they could do is wait for me." She said the final bit out loud, then took off at inhuman speed.

"Did I miss something?" Xori asked, her silver eyes wide as Tianna streaked away.

Vic tapped his temple. "Royan was heading into the

gaming area as I was coming off my shift. I gave her a heads up."

"Ah." Her soft mouth quirked into a brief smile. "Returning the favor, were you? And don't try to deny that Tianna was giving you a warning of some kind about what's in store for you today."

"Guilty as charged." He grinned at her. "Cyborg patients are a pain in the ass, huh?"

"You've been a collection of unique challenges, certainly." She brushed a strand of hair away from her face and then gestured to the door. "Shall we go in?"

Vic glanced at Ward, who stood two paces back, his hand hovering over the spot where his blaster would be if they were armed. "Wolf? You good?"

His twin nodded stiffly.

Xori moved to stand in front of Ward and looked up at the big cyborg. From Vic's position, he couldn't see her face, but he didn't need to. She'd be giving his brother one of her gentle smiles, her silver eyes full of warmth and compassion. He'd seen that expression often, both in reality and in his dreams.

"There will be nothing in that room but the three of us. I know you trust Vic with your life. Will you trust me, too?" she asked softly.

Ward nodded again, the motion a little looser this time. "I trust you."

"Good." She looked back at Vic. "Then it's time to start the next stage of your treatment."

After years of helping patients overcome their pasts, Dr. Xori Virness thought she'd seen it all. She'd treated victims of slavers, cults, and abusive mates from species and cultures all over the galaxy. She'd seen the scars left from some of the darkest acts any sentient being was capable of. Then, she'd come to the Drift and discovered the work of the Gray Men.

She despised that name. Gray indicated there was something morally nebulous about the group and their actions. There wasn't. The secretive cabal was as black as the shadows they hid in. Five of their victims were now her patients, including the two males filing into the sim-pod behind her. The door slid shut with a near-silent hiss, leaving the three of them alone in a brightly lit, white-walled room that felt far smaller than it had been when she'd shared it with Tianna.

She turned to face the twins. They stood side-by-side, forming a tall, brooding wall of pure muscle, one wearing a gray shirt, the other, navy blue.

As always, part of her was tempted to reach out and touch them. It was an impulse she would not give into. She couldn't. Not so long as they were her patients. And while Victor was moving forward with his recovery, something held Ward back. Even now, she could sense the tension in him, the way his emotions seethed like a storm trapped inside a force field. Her job was to calm that storm before containment failed, and her instincts told her she was running out of time. "I should start off by admitting this is a simple program. To protect your privacy, I learned how to do the coding myself."

Vic cocked a brow. "You taught yourself how to design sims just for us?"

"For a few of my patients, yes."

"So, what is it, exactly?" Ward asked.

"In your case, it's a digital avatar of someone who brought you both a lot of pain. Instead of talking to me about your feelings concerning this person, I thought it might be better if you could talk to them directly."

Both males froze. It was an eerie thing to witness because cyborgs became still in a way no other being could. Vic eventually exhaled and raked a hand through his hair, leaving it rumpled. "You didn't tell us that part."

"But I did tell you this would be challenging."

"You want us to talk to an avatar of *her*." Ward's tone on the last word was cold enough to freeze the surface of a star.

"I'd like you to consider it. For today, all I ask is that you stay while I activate the program. You don't need to interact with her at all."

She'd been prepared for resistance, even anger. But she'd never considered Ward's next move.

He closed the distance between them in a heartbeat, using the speed all of his kind had. He raised his hand, letting his fingers hover over a lock of her hair without quite touching. "If I do this, I want something from you."

The words sent a thrill down her spine. Not of fear. She wasn't afraid of either of them. They'd never hurt her. Despite the darkness and violence in their souls, they weren't like that. "That's not how this works. This isn't a negotiation. You know that."

He twined a strand of her hair around his finger. "I also know I'd rather suck vacuum than chat with the bitch who used us as her personal playthings for years. So, if I'm doing this, I'd like some incentive."

"What is it you want?"

He released her hair and raised his gaze to hers. "Two things."

"I'm listening."

"Wear your hair down the next time we see each other."

She nodded noncommittedly. "And the other?"

"Go out to dinner with us."

That was not what she'd expected from him. Vic had tried to ask her out a few times, but never Ward.

Vic spoke before she could. "Wolf? What the *fraxx* are you doing?"

"Moving forward. That's what we're supposed to be doing, right?" He didn't take his eyes off her. "Dinner. Hair down. Deal?"

"I don't date my patients. You know that."

He smiled. It was barely a flicker, but for one brief second, she saw past the mask to the man she was trying to help him rediscover. No sardonic comment, no over-the-top humor. Just a genuine smile. Right then, she knew she'd agree to his request. She'd do whatever it took to bring these two back from the brink of the abyss.

"We know your rules. But that means if we're ever

going to get you out on a real date, we need to get our shit together."

"You're telling me that going out to dinner with you two wouldn't be a real date?"

Victor stepped up beside his brother. "When we take you out on a proper date, you'll know it. If you say yes, we'll respect your rules. It would just be dinner."

They were double-teaming her. Working together to get their way. It was the first time they'd tried it on her, and it was harder to resist than she'd expected. Then again, almost everything about these two tempted her, despite the long, carefully itemized list of reasons she'd made as to why she shouldn't be interested. She'd even bolded and underlined the two biggest reasons. One of them was making sure she didn't get fired for taking advantage of a patient in her care...or in this case, two patients.

The list hadn't worked—her interest had only deepened—but the problem remained.

If there'd been anyone else she could trust their recovery to, she'd have stepped back as their therapist months ago. There wasn't.

"And if I say yes to dinner, then you'll both agree to three of these sim-sessions?" she asked.

And there it was again, that momentary gleam of real warmth in Ward's eyes. "Was that a counteroffer? I thought this wasn't a negotiation?"

"Three sessions," she repeated.

The two males shared a look. "You in?" Ward asked his brother.

"If you are."

"Alright then. Three." Ward held out his hand in the customary human way.

She took it, doing her best to block out the sudden surge of emotional energy that always accompanied physical contact. She got a quick flash of satisfaction and unease, but nothing more. She considered it impolite to do a deep read of other beings' emotions without their consent. Given that she had to keep her talent a secret, that meant not doing it at all.

Ward kept the handshake brief and impersonal. He'd already given away too much, but he hadn't been able to resist touching her hair. The dinner deal wasn't planned either, but he'd seen an opportunity to give Vic a chance at a little happiness. The fact he'd enjoy the outing too wasn't relevant. This was about Vic's future, not his.

He stepped away, rolling his shoulders to shake off some of the tension that was already creeping back. "What do you want us to do?"

"React honestly. Ariel Coal betrayed and abused you. Seeing her again, even as a simulation, is going to evoke strong feelings. Don't fight them."

Vic laughed. "Now I see why you asked us to come unarmed. Cyn would be pissed if we blasted holes in one of her sim-pods."

"Not just you. There's a general 'no weapons' clause in my rental contract with the Nova Club."

He looked at Vic and grinned. "Nyx?"

"Oh yeah. That one has anger issues that make us look well adjusted."

Nyx was the newest cyborg to arrive on the station, and her history was the stuff of nightmares. She'd survived years of experimentation and cruelty at the hands of the Gray Men before being rescued by the Nova Force team stationed on Astek. He and Vic had recognized her as a kindred spirit, and the three of them were forming some kind of deranged friendship. Well, four of them, really. Because wherever Nyx went, her fiancé Eric wasn't far behind.

Xori cleared her throat in gentle reproach. "You know I don't allow discussion about my other patients during sessions."

"Sorry," they said in unison.

She nodded. "Shall we proceed?"

It was one of the many qualities he found fascinating about Xori. She moved past things with a quiet calm that made it easy for everyone else to move along, too. She was tranquility personified, and just being near her could take the edge off even his darkest moods. It's why he kept coming to these sessions, despite knowing it was pointless. He was too broken to fix. All he really wanted was to hold it together long enough to see that Victor found his way out of the darkness they'd been living in.

Xori stayed in the corner nearest the door. "The simulation will appear in the center of the room. You can ask the computer to pause or end the program at any time."

"Let's get this over with," he said.

"Ready," Vic agreed.

"Computer, start program Virness-Whiskey-Foxtrot-one."

Whisky-Foxtrot. Wolf and Fox. He had just enough time to realize she'd used their nicknames when a figure appeared in the room with them - Ariel Coal. He had his hands around her throat before he took his next breath.

"You bitch!" He snarled. His grip tightened just enough he could feel her pulse racing beneath his fingers. He wanted to tear her head from her shoulders and bounce it off the walls of the room while her body twitched on the floor at his feet. Even knowing this wasn't the real thing, the urge to inflict even some small fraction of the hurt she'd done to them was almost overwhelming.

Almost, but not quite.

He eased his grip from around her neck and the simulation gasped, sucking in a lungful of air. *Veth*, the doctor had designed the hologram to react like a real person. Which meant she'd react to pain... No. He wasn't plotting that course. It didn't lead anywhere good. If he tapped into the darkness coiled tightly in his soul, he didn't know if he'd ever manage to lock it away again.

He let her go and the simulation swayed but managed to stay on its feet. "How's that for an honest —" He didn't get to finish his weak attempt at a joke, because his brother lunged at Ariel with a wordless howl of fury, grabbing her by the hair.

"Why did you do it?" He screamed, pulling the

sim's head back, so she was looking up at them. "Why did you steal our lives, Ariel? What was the *fraxxing* point of it all?"

The sim smiled, and Ward's stomach twisted in recognition. He knew that expression. Feral and cruel, it always heralded a new round of punishments and humiliations.

"I was following orders. That's all," she said.

Vic snarled. "Whose orders?"

The smile didn't leave her face as she answered, "The Gray Men, of course. You know that."

The shock of hearing her admit to it was enough to remind them both that this was a sim. Their handler had been careful to never mention who she worked for, not once in all the time they'd been dancing to her demented tune.

"You're not her." Vic released her and stepped back, his hands fisted and clamped tight to his side. "This isn't real."

Ward dropped a hand onto his twin's shoulder. "It's not real," he repeated.

Vic turned his head, and Ward tightened his grip. There was more darkness in his brother's eyes than he'd ever seen before, and it worried him. Vic was the strong one. The one who had the best chance of making it through.

"I didn't realize." He didn't elaborate. There was no need. Vic would know what he meant.

"Neither did I."

"Computer, pause program," Xori said.

The sim froze. He watched it for a second, needing

to be sure she wouldn't move if he turned his back on her. No. On *it*.

He sucked in a deep breath and moved the same time Vic did, both of them pivoting to face Xori.

"But you knew, didn't you, doctor?" Vic asked, his words clipped.

Xori nodded. "That you were still angry? Yes, I knew."

"But he was getting better," Ward protested.

"You're *both* improving. Not being angry isn't the goal. We're all angry about things in our past. It's what you do with those feelings that's important." She held out her hands, palms up. "There's an old human adage that I'd like you to think about. Each of us has two wolves inside us."

"I like this story already," Ward murmured.

"You would. Why are there never foxes in these stories?" Vic grumbled.

Xori shook her head, a small smile touching her lips. "They could be foxes if you'd like. The point is, there are two animals fighting for dominance within us. One represents all our darkest feelings: anger, sorrow, regret, arrogance. The other stands for the best parts of us: hope, peace, kindness, and love. The animal that wins this fight is the one we choose to feed."

She looked at Vic. "Pretending one of the foxes isn't there isn't a solution." She turned to Ward. "We have to be aware of both sides and then decide which one to nurture."

Was that what Vic had been doing?

Ward gave an inward sigh. If that was true, then he

would need to stick around a little longer. He couldn't move on until he was sure Vic was going to be alright without him. Getting him together with Xori was part of the plan. They'd make a good team. Take care of each other. It had taken him a while to see it, but now he knew what he needed to do. First, he'd make sure Vic was happy. Then, he could walk away and leave him to his new, better life.

CHAPTER TWO

Dinner. *Not a date. Just dinner.*

She would keep telling herself that until she believed it, because that's all it could be. Humans still had some oddly rigid rules when it came to relationships in general, but those rules were even more inflexible when it came to bonds between doctors and those in their care. If Ward and Victor were Pheran, it wouldn't be an issue, but they weren't. They were human, so she was doing her best to abide by human guidelines. Especially since the human's Interstellar Armed Forces were paying a good portion of her salary right now. Making them unhappy was not a good idea. In fact, it probably ranked right up there with poking a *chorzet* nest or insulting a Jeskyran's brood mother.

This was just dinner, and she'd only agreed to it because it had ensured the brothers made it through their first virtual encounter with their former handler. They might be physically identical, but they were coping with their trauma in different ways. This had been good for both of them.

She finished dressing and added an ornate bronze cuff to one of her ears. It wasn't something she wore at work, but it made things easier when out in public. It was a token of her social caste, reassuring any other Pherans she met that she was permitted to be out on her own. Some aspects of her culture had traveled with her species, even to places as remote as the Drift.

She'd chosen to wear one of her favorite outfits, a simple sheath dress of black with hints of gold along the hem and sleeves. She draped the matching shawl around her shoulders – the airflow on Astek station was notoriously inconsistent – brushed her hair one last time and declared herself presentable.

She was looking forward to tonight. Date or not, she didn't get many opportunities to go out. Her work kept her busy and being in public meant she needed to guard herself against the constant background of emotional turbulence that accompanied any public outing. She'd learned how to manage her gift years ago, but it could still be taxing.

She checked the time and swore softly. She needed to go. Since she'd started taking on patients with connections to the human's military, she'd been offered quarters within Nova Force's section of the station - for her own protection. Security was tightening all over the station these days, in part because of the upcoming gala, but also because of the recent discovery that the Gray Men had paid operatives on Astek.

She'd agreed to the housing offer because it was

safer, convenient, and as bonus, they'd arranged for her to have office space nearby. The only downside was that security was so tight that getting anyone past the guard posts was usually more trouble than it was worth. Because of that, she'd suggested they meet at her office, which was only a short walk away.

The guards nodded to her as she passed the security checkpoint. The corridor beyond them was relatively quiet. Most of the denizens of the station avoided the military outpost that had appeared in their midst a few months ago. Neither side was entirely comfortable with the arrangement, and tensions ran high these days, a fact she was painfully aware of every time she walked the decks of the station.

Her office was in the buffer zone between the two, a short stretch of corridor full of offices much like hers. Small businesses who didn't rely on foot traffic and often had links to IAF or Nova Force.

Even from here, the raucous clamor of the main promenade could be heard. Vendor's cries blended with music of all kinds that rose and fell in volume as the patrons of various establishments came and went.

Two figures walked toward her, perfectly matched in height, build, and gait. Their hair was even styled the same tonight, the dark brown length tied back into a tail. Even so, she could tell them apart. There were subtle differences in their body language, and Ward had a habit of walking a half pace behind his brother so their shoulders overlapped just a little.

Both wore black pants and military-style boots, and she noted with amusement they were both armed with blasters at their hip and a combat knife tucked into their belts. "Are you planning on killing our dinner yourselves?" she asked, not bothering to raise her voice.

Vic didn't respond until he was only a few feet away. Then he grinned and shrugged, the motion drawing the charcoal fabric of his shirt tight across his "That wasn't the plan, but if you ask us to, you know we'll make it happen."

"I don't think that will be necessary."

"Glad to hear it, because I wouldn't recommend eating anything roaming free on this station." Ward gave a dramatic shudder. "Too many legs."

She had to agree. While the station's condition had been improving lately, there were still vast stretches of maintenance conduits where pest species from across the known galaxy managed to thrive, and in some cases grow to nightmarish proportions. "So, if we're not foraging for our meal, where are we going?"

To her surprise, Ward stepped up and offered her his arm, Pheran fashion, palm down, his forearm perfectly level with his elbow. "We are going to a little place called the *Dobna Brin*."

She took his arm with a small smile of thanks, resting her fingers lightly on his sleeve, just above his wrist. "Isn't that Torski for something like 'bowl of comfort?' Sounds promising."

Vic chuckled as he set off toward the noise of the concourse. "Told you."

"Have I mentioned today that smug is not a good look for you?" Ward grumbled, but she could sense he wasn't actually displeased.

"So, how many languages do you speak?" Ward asked.

"A few. Several dialects of Pheran, Galactic Standard, obviously, and I've picked up a fair bit of Torski through the years. The one I can't wrap my brain around is Jeskyran. I know enough to argue with a vendor when they try to cheat me, but that's all."

Ward turned his head and tapped his temple with his free hand. "We're programmed to understand every language in the galaxy, and Jeskyran still gives me a headache. It's all those click consonants."

The noise level rose as they approached the main concourse. When the crowd thickened, her escorts shifted positions so that Vic was partially in front of her and to her right while Ward stayed on her left. Between them they created a protective shield that allowed her to move unmolested through the throng. Their thoughtfulness had an unintended side-effect – the emotional noise emanating from the crowd was muted enough it took almost no effort to block it out.

They took one of the bullet trains that crisscrossed the station. The cars were cramped and carried a lingering reek of body odor, stale food, and even staler air. They had to rush to find seating as a robotic voice intoned a list of instructions. Clear the doors. No food. No fighting. All passengers must remain seated while the train is in motion.

They were moving before the recording looped a third time.

It was pointless to try and talk. Holographic displays shimmered into existence over every seat, blaring advertisements for everything from pleasure sims to the latest advancements in combat weaponry. The brothers took turns swatting away the more graphic ads, sending tiny naked forms flying in various directions. For a fee, you could block the ads above your seat, but most beings didn't bother. That only meant you'd be bombarded by the digital billboards of everyone who didn't pay.

She was giggling by the time they reached their stop, and once they were outside, she burst into a fit of full-blown laughter. "*Veth.* You, with the—" she flicked her hand to the left. "And then she flew right through the window… And the green one! I swear she was winking at you, Ward."

"Jealous?" Ward asked her.

"Of pixels? Never," she retorted.

"Not even green ones?" Vic asked. He was grinning at his brother, who looked like he wanted this entire conversation diverted to the center of the nearest star.

"Definitely not green ones. They're not even ripe yet and likely taste terrible. Now, if she'd been blue…" she trailed off as she registered the impact of her joke.

Neither male was laughing. They were, however, staring.

"Did she…?" Ward asked.

"I think so." Vic reached out to take her hand, running his thumb across her knuckles. "Are you telling us you're ripe for the picking, Xori Virness?"

Her breath caught in her throat. The weight of their stares so heavy she swore someone had turned up the gravity. That hadn't been what she'd meant. *Or was it?*

The denial she'd been about to utter melted away unspoken. "I honestly don't know."

Vic's fingers tightened around hers for a brief second. "When you do, be sure to tell us, hmm?"

He released her hand, but the air between the three of them still hummed like they were standing too close to an unshielded energy conduit.

"I will."

"Good," Ward offered her his arm again, the act just as formal as before, but this time the barely-there connection of her fingers against his forearm filled her awareness. His sleeve had slid up his arm, exposing bare skin. Every time she grazed against it, she caught glimmers of emotions too powerful for her to ignore. Regret. Amusement. Affection. Desire. The feelings winked in and out like a pulsar.

She let them lead her through the crowd without really noting where they were going. The main concourse was as busy here as in the sector they'd come from. The calls of vendors and promoters were just as raucous, the sights and sounds as vibrant and jarring, but she floated along in a fugue, her mind whirling with the implications of what she'd said a moment ago.

At first, it had been easy to ignore the attraction she felt towards the two big males. It was purely physical, a reaction to their good looks and obvious strength. Then it had deepened into something more. The *haja*, the attraction between the healer and the ones seeking healing. She'd disregarded that, too, because of the human's rules and her own. This though... this was something more, or it could be if she let it. There were just so many reasons it wasn't a good idea.

~

He was supposed to be doing this for Vic, not himself. The plan was to bring Xori into their lives so that she could take Ward's place when he stepped back and let the shadows take him. His brain clearly hadn't gotten the message, though, because he was enjoying having Xori with them. She was easy company, and just being around her made the world a little lighter. Maybe that was it. There wasn't much light in his life. He had his little family of batch-siblings, along with Dana and Mya, the chubby-fisted twins with their silver eyes full of trust he hadn't earned. And, for tonight, at least, he had Xori.

He glanced down at the slender female beside him, acutely aware of the gentle brush of her fingertips against his skin. It was the first time she'd ever touched him, and the brief contact had kindled a fire that threatened to turn his carefully laid plans to ash. As much as he wanted her, he didn't deserve her. She brought a little light into his world, but all he could offer her in return was a soul as black and cold as the void outside.

They reached the little café he and Vic had stumbled upon by accident one night. Neither of them slept much, so exploring the station in what passed for nights out here had become a common pastime.

The *Dobna Brin* was one of their favorite

destinations. The Torski family that ran it was a poly grouping with enough spouses and offspring to allow them to keep it open around the clock, making it a perfect place to go when the walls of their quarters closed in around them.

Tagor boomed out a welcome the moment he saw them at the door. "Ah, Rezka, our wanderers are back for another visit. Come in, come in. Your usual spot?"

"Something a little bigger, this time, Tag. We've brought a friend."

The big Torski's brows almost vanished into his shaggy crop of blue-black hair as Xori stepped out from behind his brother. She looked like a child's doll compared to the massive bulk of the heavy-worlder, and an unexpected urge to pull her back to his side struck him like a rogue comet. Ahead of him, Vic's hand twitched as if he were fighting the same protective need, which made Ward feel a little better. Apparently, he wasn't the only one feeling this way.

Tagor bowed his head. "A pleasure."

Xori raised her hands in a gesture Ward couldn't make out. Then she said, "Prosperity and blessings to you and your family," in Tagor's own language.

Tagor's boom laughing filled the air. "A gem! You have brought a rare and shining jewel to dine with us tonight. Come, come, Rezka has already found a place for you."

One of Tag's wives smiled and pointed to a booth near the back of the little shop.

"This one is best for privacy," Reska told them as they took a seat in the U-shaped booth. She was beaming as she pointed out the terminal with the menu and screen controls. It was for Xori's benefit, but he still wanted to tell the Torksi female to go away so they could enjoy a little of the privacy she'd been extolling just a moment before.

Once they were alone, Vic activated the privacy screen, a far simpler version of the same tech the military used. There was a low hum and the air across the open end of the booth appeared to thicken and shimmer. Vic touched the controls again, and the view from inside the booth cleared so they could see the restaurant once more.

"I take it you come here a lot." Xori was already parsing through the menu as she spoke.

"Good food, quiet spot. Yeah, we like it here," Vic said.

"I guessed you'd eat most of your meals at the Nova Club. The food there is excellent."

Ward nodded. "It is, but it's also our home and our workplace."

Vic continued the explanation. "And our entire family is there."

"All. The. Time," Ward finished the thought.

Xori sat back, smiling.

"What?" Ward asked.

"You finished each other's thoughts," she said.

"Well, yeah. We've always done that." The words were out of his mouth before he realized that wasn't true. Not recently.

"It was one of the things you said you used to do. Before. I've never heard you do it."

Before. A small word that encompassed a lifetime. She was right, though. It was one of the many things they'd lost while under the thrall of their cold-hearted bitch of a handler.

"Well, hell. Now you mention it, I think that's the first time in a while." Vic reached behind Xori to slap Ward's shoulder. "We're getting our shit together."

"Looks like." And if it were true, then it was yet another sign that Xori was the one. Who better to share their lives with than the one who had given it back to them?

Meals at the *Dobna Brin* were meant to be leisurely social affairs. An array of various vat-grown proteins and pressed vegetable matter were available to order. The ingredients were then delivered to the table on trays, along with a massive bowl of broth that came with its own heater tucked in beneath it. The food was skewered and cooked in the broth, while the diners grazed on bread and spicy wedges of fried tubers.

After their meal was ordered and the drinks were delivered, the conversation fell into a lull that threatened to become an awkward silence.

"You look nice tonight," he said, then immediately realized his mistake. This wasn't supposed to be a date. Compliments were date territory, weren't they? "Uh, I mean. You always look nice. Professional. But there's something different..." he trailed off and silently wondered why the *fraxx* no one had thought to include a subprogram about small talk along with all the military knowledge they'd crammed into his head.

Xori smoothed her hair back from her ear. "You mean my *matyri*?"

He took the lifeline she tossed him. "Yeah. That's new. It's pretty. Why don't you wear it more often?"

Her lips pressed together for a brief moment. It was barely more than a micro-expression, but it spoke volumes.

"You don't need to talk about it if you don't want to," Vic said. He'd caught her reaction, too.

"You've both opened up to me about your lives." She dropped one shoulder in the Pheran version of a shrug and then touched a slender finger to her chest, just above her heart. "If we are to become real friends, you deserve the same from me."

He hadn't planned on it, but somehow his fingers were brushing over the bronze adornment and skimming the delicate tuft of hair at the top of her ear. "Okay. So what is this?"

She shivered, and the deep blue of her stripes got even darker for a moment. Was she ticklish? A thought stirred at the back of his mind. Ears weren't ticklish, but they were sensitive. In humans, they could be an erogenous zone—oh ho. He withdrew his hand and filed that bit of information away for later.

She paused to take several sips of her cocktail, leaned back with a sigh, and glanced between them. "I don't like this seating arrangement. I can't see you both at the same time, and to talk to one of you, I have to turn my back on the other."

"I can fix that, with your permission?" Ward said.

"What are you up to?" his brother queried on their internal channel.

He ignored the question. Vic might be programmed to take the lead in most things, but for some reason he wasn't ready to move on Xori. That meant it was up to him.

"If you have a solution to this problem, I'm willing," Xori said.

"Hang onto your drink." He pushed the table out with one foot, then reached over and carefully picked her up. He placed her on his lap so that she was sitting across his thighs, facing Vic. "There. Now you can see us both."

"Ward!" Xori protested.

"Call me Wolf."

"I'm going to call you *something* in a second. Put me down. This isn't appropriate."

"You gave me permission," he pointed out.

She huffed and waved her hands in graceful little circles. "I thought you'd move around to sit by Vic or well, anything but this."

"It's like she doesn't know us at all," He deadpanned to his brother, who burst out laughing in response.

"I don't know whether to be indignant on her behalf or pissed I didn't think of it first," Vic sent over their link.

"The second one. If she were truly unhappy, she would have let us know by now." And as much as she was protesting, Xori hadn't made any attempt to move away. She'd stayed nestled in his arms, a fact that

pleased him more than it should. This beautiful, delicate female didn't fear him, and she knew him better than anyone else on the station. Well, anyone but Vic.

"And now you're talking to each other on that private channel of yours. You know my rule about that."

Vic leaned forward, and there was something predatory in his eyes that Ward hadn't seen since *before*. "Those are your rules for the office. We're not in a session right now. So, I don't think the rules apply."

"This is not a date," she reminded them.

"This time, no," Ward said.

"Next time, though…" Vic added.

"There's going to be a next time?" Xori's tone was softer now.

"That's up to you," Vic said.

"But we want that," Ward said.

Xori glanced at him, then looked to Vic. "Maybe."

Vic steepled his hands in front of him the way Xori often did, and his next words came out in a high, fluting tone that was as close to hers as his brother could manage. "I think we've made excellent progress today."

"I do not sound like that!" Xori protested with a laugh.

"Nope, your voice is a lot nicer to listen to than his." He pointed to Vic, who grabbed his glass and raised it. "You're a lot nicer to look at, too." He took a sip, then inclined his head to her. "I still want to know about your *matyri*, though."

She raised a hand to the interwoven lines of bronze

on her ear. "This is the reason I'm allowed to be here at all."

His hold on her tightened just a little. Why wouldn't she be allowed to be here with them? "Explain."

"I am *sooran-nah*, which is the lowest caste in our society."

"Pherans have a caste system? I didn't know that," Vic said.

"We do. It's not something we talk about openly." Her shoulder dropped into a subtle shrug.

"Why not?" Ward asked.

"Because most of the Pherans you have ever met are from the lower caste. We're free to leave our planet if we can find the means to pay for it. We're the labor force for our society, and with all the automation and technology we have, the supply far exceeds the demand."

He was chewing that over when their food arrived, and the next few minutes were spent showing Xori how to skewer her meal and place it in the pot to cook. He was gratified to note she stayed in his lap the whole time. As far as he was concerned, she could stay there for the rest of the night.

"You said the lower caste Pherans are free to leave. Does that mean the others can't?" Vic asked once they were settled again.

"It depends. High caste males, yes. Females? No. Not often, and never unescorted, though that can vary depending on how progressive her immediate family is. Some parts of my homeworld have made an effort to set aside the caste system. Most have not."

"That has to do with the fact your species' females need to be protected, right?" Ward asked.

Xori snorted. "How many Pheran females have you met that fit the meek and gentle stereotype? Zura is half Pheran, and I wouldn't call her meek unless I had a running head start."

"You're gentle. And Zura's half-human, from seriously insane stock. You have met her brother, right?" Vic pointed out.

"I have, and your point is well taken, but the females of the lower castes aren't really meek. that's an affectation we adopt to avoid giving offense to the higher ranks of society."

He thought about the female Pherans he'd met over the years, most of them here on Astek station. Xori was right. They'd all been pleasant enough, but nothing about them had really fit the stereotype. He just hadn't noticed. "What happens if you offend someone?"

Xori tensed, and Ward placed a hand on her back. He'd meant it as a comfort, but the moment his fingers touched her hair, the motion turned into in a slow caress. "If I was back on Phera Prime, then I might be arrested or fined. It would depend on the insult given, and the rank of the other party."

"That's insane," both he and Vic said at the same time.

The subtle shrug again, this time matched to a tossing-away gesture he hadn't seen her use before. "That is the Pheran way. Which is why I no longer live where such things are an issue." She touched her *matyri*. "This tells any other members of my culture my social standing and situation at a glance. It makes things simpler."

"And here I thought that humans had the monopoly on prejudice and stupid social rules," Vic muttered.

Xori laughed. "I have yet to meet any species that enlightened. You just don't see the Pheran system because you're not part of it."

That thought kept rolling around his head as they ate and talked, peppering Xori with questions about life on Phera Prime. She'd shared her stories openly and honestly, and by the time the meal was done Ward felt like he knew her much better, and he liked everything he'd learned. He also knew that she was stronger than he'd realized. Not that it changed anything. Strong or gentle, she was one of the best things in their lives, and he felt a powerful need to protect her from anything that might dim her smile.

CHAPTER THREE

BY THE TIME they were headed home, Xori was experiencing a pleasant buzz that made her feel like the gravity was slightly lower than usual. It wasn't the liquor she'd had with dinner, though. It was the kind of high that came from good food and better company. She was always reminding her patients to build connections with other beings and make sure to enjoy the small pleasures of life, but somehow, she'd failed to take her own advice. Laughter, friendship, and even physical contact hadn't been part of her life since coming to the Drift. She looked at the two handsome males escorting her, their long strides adjusted to keep pace with hers.

Not until tonight.

They were headed to the waystation to catch a bullet train back to their sector, but she wasn't ready for their night out to end. "Would you like to walk instead?"

The main concourse was quieter now, and the

brothers on either side of her, taking advantage of the extra space.

"I hate those trains. Walking is better," Ward stated.

"And we'd get to spend more time with you," Vic agreed.

"Then it's a good thing I wore comfortable shoes." She gestured around them. "Now comes the point where I admit I have no idea where we are. So, which way do we go?"

Ward pointed back in the direction they'd come with a jerk of his thumb. "That way."

They both offered her their arms, and instead of choosing one, she placed a hand on each of theirs. She smiled as she caught a glimmer of male pride and satisfaction from them. She left the connection open for a few extra seconds, reading more of their emotions without dipping beneath the surface. They were relaxed and happy. More so than she'd ever sensed from either of them before.

In the back of her mind, a little voice whispered a smug 'I told you so.' She ignored it, for now.

They strolled and chatted about anything and everything, the conversation flowing between topics that ranged from the rules of starburst, an elaborate game played in the Nova's casino, to the guest list for the corporate gala Astek Corporation was hosting in a matter of weeks.

They showed her parts of the station she'd never been to before, though her escorts seemed to know every meter of the place. They navigated the light crowds with total confidence, sharing bits of information about the occasional restaurant, bar, or specialty shop.

"You're going to need to draw me a map so I can find my way back here. I had no idea I could get Pheran ingredients for my food dispenser on this station."

"No map needed. We'll bring you whenever you'd like," Vic replied.

"All we do is work and talk about our *fraxxing* feelings with this therapist we know. We've got plenty of time to take you shopping," Ward added.

"Thank you. I'd enjoy that, but only if you let me buy you lunch afterward."

"You don't need to do that," Vic protested.

"No. But I want to." She turned to look up at him. "Please?"

Ward laughed. "She's giving you *the look*, isn't she?"

She looked at Ward. "What look?"

His mouth turned down at the corners and he opened his eyes wide until he looked like a child who'd been told they couldn't have any more sweets. "This one."

"I do not look like that!"

"You're right. When he does it all I want to do is smack him. When you look at us that way? We'd rearrange the stars themselves if you asked." Vic said.

They moved at the same time, stepping in front of her, each of them holding out a hand. It was so fluid it had to have been coordinated, but something told her it wasn't. This was what they were like when they were in synch with each other. It was a glimpse of who they'd been before, and what they could be again.

She didn't know what to say, so she opted to say nothing as she took their offered hands. They fell in beside her without a word, leading her along the concourse as if nothing had changed — but it had.

A few minutes later they stepped into the largest open space she'd seen since coming to Astek. The area was at least three decks high, possibly more, and the dull metal ceiling was partially covered by massive screens that showed what she assumed was the view beyond the station. Scaffolding climbed the walls, and crews were busy installing more of the screens. When the project was done, it would turn the entire roof into one vast viewport.

"What's this?" she asked, letting go of their hands to gesture around them.

"This is the main hub for travelers coming off the luxury passenger vessels," Ward told her.

"Ah. That explains the facelift. They're prepping for the party."

"Yeah." Ward scowled. "But there are other parts of the station that need more than just a fresh coat of paint and some snazzy new tech. People see this, they'll start wondering why a pretty view is more important than repairing the air recyclers in the lower residential areas."

"Maybe you should point that out to her the next time you see her? Suggest that she do some sort of visible improvement elsewhere?"

Vic nodded. "Or we could drop a hint to Royan and Owen. They're like the unofficial ambassadors between we lowly folk and our corporate landlord."

"Better them than us," Ward said.

"Tianna is more than your landlord, though. She's a friend and a fellow cyborg, isn't she?"

Vic glanced down at her in surprise. "Well, yeah. But she's also the daughter of one of the assholes who bribed their way around the rules and built themselves armies of flesh-and-blood toy soldiers so they could play wargames."

"And that's her fault?"

"I…" Vic sighed. "I know she's as much a victim as we are in some ways. But sometimes it's hard to remember that when I see crap like this happening. I want to fight back somehow, and the corporations are an obvious target."

"And you were created to be soldiers. Identifying threats and then dealing with them is hardwired into your psyches. I know. But you're more than your programming. Never forget that."

They both nodded, and the three of them set off again. The silence between them lingered, dampening some of her enjoyment, and neither of them took her hand again. She missed the connection, but not enough to reach for them. Not yet.

A swelling wave of noise rose up behind them, and she glanced back, curious. A flow of new arrivals poured into the area from a door that must lead to the docking ring.

A whoop of pleasure rang out, and as she watched, two Vardarians took to the air. It was the first time she'd seen that species in flight, and she stopped to watch, awestruck, as the male and female wheeled and soared overhead, clearly delighted to be able to stretch their wings after their journey.

Someone ran into her from behind, and she staggered forward a few steps before regaining her balance. She turned in that direction and found herself looking into the outraged face of a Pheran male. She didn't even have to look at his matyri to know he was *taryn-nah*, the highest caste. She could see it every detail from his clothes to his stance.

"Unclean vermin. You dare to touch me?" He shouted at her in Pheran. She dropped her gaze and raised her hands, palms up, wrists together, in a gesture of supplication she hadn't had to use in years.

The male lashed out with a booted foot, catching her on the side of her knee. It gave way and she fell, biting back a cry she knew would only draw more of the male's ire.

Someone caught her mid-fall and a familiar voice said, "I've got you."

She didn't know which one of them had her until Ward strode past her.

"You bastard!" he bellowed, and the Pheran took a step back in shock, but Ward kept coming, his fury hammering against her awareness, raw, primal, and completely uncontrolled.

Time slowed to a crawl.

If he drew a weapon or used even a fraction of his cyborg strength against the other male, the Pheran would die. She had to stop him.

She scrambled to her feet, freeing herself from Vic's grasp, and dove for Ward. She needed to be as close as possible if this had any chance of working.

Please let this work.

How had such an amazing evening gone to hell so fast?

Ward hadn't even realized Xori had fallen behind until it was too late. He'd heard the shouts, looked down to check on her, and felt a sickening twist in his gut when he saw the gap between him and Vic. She was gone.

They'd spun around in time to see everything, but not soon enough to stop it from happening. The vicious tone, the cruel words, the assault on the female they should have been protecting. The noise of the crowd faded and his focus narrowed until all he could see was the Pheran who'd dared to lash out at Xori.

The two of them moved together, training and years of fighting side-by-side making communication unnecessary. Vic went to catch Xori while Ward faced down the asshole who'd hurt her.

Anger poured through him, turning the warm glow of contentment into something different – a conflagration of fury. His rage was as hot and bright as rocket fuel at the moment of ignition. The blue bastard would pay. Hurting someone just because he could, because he thought his position gave him the right. It was wrong, and this time, he was free to step in and put a stop to it.

He went after the other male, hands fisted to stop himself going for either blaster or knife. Too quick. Too clean. He raised a hand to strike him, and then everything changed.

It was like walking into a sunbeam after spending countless days trapped in darkness. Light poured through him, banishing every shadow and filling him with a sense of peace and contentment that was painfully, impossibly pure.

Something soft and warm hit him from behind, and he spun around to find Xori there, unsteady on her feet, her silver eyes bright with tears. She touched his hand, wrapping her fingers around his fist. "Don't. You don't need to hurt him."

He took in a breath so deep his ribs creaked, her voice resonating through him like the chime of a silver bell.

"Are you alright?" he asked., still dazed from the emotional transformation.

"I am. But I want to go home, now. Please?"

He unclenched his fingers to take her hand, and Vic appeared in his vision, staring at something behind him. The Pheran. Holy *fraxx*. He'd turned his back on a threat. He gave his head a shake, trying to make sense of what he'd just experienced. The sudden shift in mood had shaken him, left him emotionally off-kilter. He wanted to regain the momentary flash of peace he'd felt, but it was already fading away. He let it go. There were more important things to deal with right now.

Vic pointed at the male Ward had been ready to beat to death. "This is over. And if you ever do harm to a female of any species on this station again, we'll find you and make sure you regret it. You're not on Phera Prime now. Your rules don't apply here."

The Pheran snarled, a sound that lacked any real venom. "Are you threatening me, human?"

"No. Just stating facts, Pheran." Vic's tone was colder than the void outside.

Xori took Vic's hand and tugged at it. She hadn't let a single tear fall, but he could see she was hurting and unhappy. "I want to go home." The words were sharper now, edged with tears and pain that neither of them could resist.

Vic turned to her and nodded. "Home."

Vic's voice sounded inside his head. *"What happened? I thought you were going to kill him. Then you just… stopped."*

Ward leaned down and swung Xori into his arms, cradling her slender body against his. *"I don't know. I was furious. Then, I wasn't. I can't explain it."* But he'd sell what was left of his soul to experience that moment of perfect peace again.

"I'm alright. I can walk," Xori said, but there was no real note of protest in her voice, and she didn't try to push herself out of his arms.

"You're not walking on that leg until you get it checked out by a doctor."

She surprised him by laughing, though the sound had a brittle quality to it, like ice rattling in an empty glass. "I *am* a doctor."

Vic shot her a frustrated look. "Then Ward will carry

you until we find someplace quiet so you can assess yourself properly."

"Then I'm going to close my eyes and try not to think about everyone staring at me right now." She did just that, her head tipping to rest on his shoulder.

"You do what you need to. We'll get you out of here." He dipped his head to nuzzle her cheek ever so briefly, the only comfort he could offer without crossing any lines.

"Thank you."

She was pulling away from them, he could feel it. All the warmth and wonder of the evening was gone now, and he was standing on the edge of the abyss again. He still didn't understand what had happened back there, but he'd figure it out eventually. He had to. Because if there was a way to drive out the darkness in him, then it should work on Vic. His brother could be happy again. That's all Ward wanted.

On the way back, they both tried to get her to agree to go to the med-center, but she refused. Every time they pushed, she withdrew a little farther into herself, so they stopped, hoping to salvage at least some of the progress they'd made. Ward wanted to track down the *fraxxing* blue bastard and kick his ass for not only hurting Xori, but screwing up what had been a good night, one of the best he could remember.

In the end, they stopped at her office and set her down in the waiting room while she'd checked herself over. It wasn't a large space. There were only two chairs and a small, battered reception desk facing the door. There wasn't even a chair behind it, because Xori relied on a basic AI system to manage her patients.

Xori sat in one of the chairs, her leg stretched out in front of her, the hem of her dress hitched up to bare her legs to the knee. Normally, he'd be enjoying the view of her shapely calves and the striped markings that crisscrossed her limbs and vanished beneath the fabric, but not tonight. All he could see right now were the bruises blooming on her skin. She'd been hurt on their watch, and that didn't sit well with him. Not at all.

"See? Just a little bruising. No swelling or anything to worry about. I told you. There are some mild pain-blockers in my office. I'll take some now." Xori got to her feet and both he and Vic moved to help her, but she shook her head and gestured for them to stay away. "I'm fine. See? Walking on my own and everything."

"If it still hurts tomorrow, will you please go see Dr. Jefferies at the center?" Vic asked.

The door to her office opened and she walked out of sight before answering. "I'll go if I think I need to."

"*Stubborn,*" he sent the thought to Vic.

"*And pulling away from us. How do we fix this?*"

"*By being more stubborn than she is.*"

Vic nodded in agreement. Lately they hadn't always been in the same orbit, but this was different. This was Xori.

She reappeared a few minutes later and gave them an airy smile that didn't quite reach her eyes. "See? All better."

"Better or not, we're still walking you to the checkpoint," Ward informed her.

"Or your quarters, if you'd let us."

"It's not necessary. And a little exercise will help get rid of any lingering stiffness."

He had no idea if that was true or not. Between his cybernetic enhancements and the nanotech coursing through his blood, his body could rapidly heal anything short of a direct hit from a blaster at close range. He could also block pain at will, an ability he wished he could share with Xori right now. He hated seeing her hurting, and despite her efforts, he knew she was. He could see it in the way she held herself and the micro-expressions she was doing her best to hide.

"It's your choice," Vic conceded.

"And we'll respect it," Ward stepped in and offered her his arm. "But that doesn't mean we like it."

She flashed him a tiny but genuine smile, then settled her hand on his forearm. "Noted."

It was all he could do not to bend down and kiss her, or pull her into his arms and hold her until all the stiffness melted away.

She must have sensed it because her eyes widened and she leaned back from him a little.

Vic moved to the door, triggering it to open, then flung out one hand in an overly dramatic gesture. "Shall we?"

Xori relaxed again. "Indeed, we shall."

They walked the short distance to the checkpoint in silence. It wasn't the way he'd wanted this evening to end. Next time, they'd have to do better.

CHAPTER FOUR

XORI WAS HIDING FROM THEM, and it was pissing him off.

Victor stomped through the staff-only entrance to the backrooms of the Nova Club. The thumping music and the incessant drone of the crowd cutting off as soon as the door slid shut behind him. He exhaled and let the relative quiet wash over him, trying to smooth away at least some of the tension that crackled around him since Xori had canceled their next appointment.

By text message, no less.

That had been two days ago, and she'd ignored every attempt to contact her. She had just been in the club, doing a sim-pod session with one of her other patients. He knew that because Jaeger—who by some strange twist of fate had gone from his subordinate soldier to his supervisor—had made it clear that he and Ward needed to stay in the gaming area for the past hour. That had never happened before, and there was only one reason it was happening now.

Xori didn't want to see them.

He stalked through the corridors, heading for their quarters and a shower to wash away the lingering scent of booze and food that clung to the place no matter how well the air-scrubbers were functioning.

Ward's shift didn't end for a few more hours, which meant he had a little time to himself. Maybe he'd go for a walk, check in with Corp-Sec and see if that asshole Pheran had been behaving himself. They hadn't filed a formal complaint, but he'd given his friends Mack and Dash a heads up about what happened and they'd noted it in case there were further issues. The odds of Xori crossing paths with the high-ranking jerk were low, but if it did… his hand closed into a fist and bounced off his thigh a few times before he realized what he was doing and forced himself to exhale. Getting worked up wasn't going to solve anything.

Xori was only one of his problems. Ward was the other one. They'd talked about what he'd experienced, the sudden transition from anger to calm, the momentary sense of utter peace. And every time they spoke of it, his brother's voice held a note of longing he'd never heard before. It worried him.

They both believed Xori was involved. She had to be, but neither of them understood how she'd done it, draining Ward's fury before he could do something there'd be no coming back from. She'd saved him from himself. But if she could do that, then why hadn't she done it before? Why were they struggling to heal themselves when she could have fixed them months ago? He had too many questions, and the only one with the answers was hiding from them.

He turned and started back down the drab corridor he'd just come from, his boots ringing on the dented floor as he picked up the pace. At some point in the last few seconds, he'd made a decision. She might not want to speak with them, yet, but he needed to talk to her. They'd been on the brink of something special the other night. He wanted to pursue that and get the answers he and Ward needed. It didn't matter if she wasn't ready to face them. Her time was up.

Xori made the walk back to her office faster than usual, ignoring the occasional twinge from her still-healing knee. Since the incident with the Pheran male, her anxiety kicked up every time she ventured into the station. She felt vulnerable in a way she hadn't in years, and she hated it, even if it was only temporary. Her fear, like the bruise on her leg, would fade eventually. She'd make sure of it.

What wasn't going away any time soon was the situation with Ward and Victor. Not that she regretted what she'd done. Draining Ward's anger before he did something there was no coming back from had been the right thing to do. But now, she didn't know what to say to them.

She snorted in frustration and leaned back in her chair. Some therapist she was, hiding in her office, avoiding two of her patients. She couldn't go on this way, but she had no idea how to move forward. Nothing had changed. The human rules for therapists and patients still applied. They were still different species. Not to mention that as cyborgs, Vic and Ward's lifespans would likely be calculated in centuries instead of decades. What kind of life could they have when only one of them aged? And then there were her secrets. The only beings in existence who knew what she could do were her parents. It was the only way to stay free.

The females of her family had hidden their talents for four generations, now. They taught their daughters the skills and control they'd need from the time they were small, preparing for the day they'd be tested. It was a test no one wanted to pass. Those with the gift of *m'bara* were taken from their families and forbidden to ever contact them again. They were *Nazeela Ulo,* Treasures of the People, Precious commodities to be gifted to the powerful. They became prized tools instead of free beings, bound by Pheran law to a lifetime of service and duty. If any Pheran learned what she could do, she'd be torn out of her life and returned to her homeworld to join the handful of others who shared her gifts.

She shuddered — the male who had attacked her simply because she was of lesser status and was in his way. She would never go back to that life.

She closed her eyes and took several slow, cleansing breaths, seeking answers to the same questions she'd been playing on a loop since that night. Was she really thinking about changing her relationship with Vic and Ward? Would they even want to see her again once they knew what she could do? Could she trust them with her secret? She knew the answer to at least one of her questions, but knowing she wanted to be with the twins only led to more considerations. If she agreed to go out with them, she'd have to tell them the truth. If she did that, she was certain they'd never speak about her abilities. But if they knew she could take away their pain, would they forgive her for not doing it before? Would they believe she never read them during their sessions? What would it be like to be with them? How would the others react? Would she lose her rooms and office if the IAF didn't approve? Was she really considering being with two males at once?

She rubbed her temple, feeling a headache coming on. She had to figure things out before she spoke to Vic and Ward again. She just hoped they would understand she needed a little time.

Her reception AI pinged, indicating someone had entered the waiting room. She frowned and called up her schedule, a holographic display popping into existence above her desk just as someone hammered on the door to her office.

"Xori! I know you're in there. Open this *fraxxing* door, please. I need to talk to you."

"You don't have an appointment!" She called back, relaxing a little as she realized the familiar voice outside had to belong to Victor. The word *please* wasn't one Ward used often, and never when he was mad.

"I don't have an appointment because you canceled it!"

"I said I'd reschedule you for next week."

"I need to talk to you *now*, Xori. It's about Ward."

She sighed, the weight of his words pressing down on her like she was being crushed beneath some divine being's thumb. She'd hoped for more time to figure out what to tell them, and how to manage whatever fallout followed. It wasn't going to happen that way.

She touched a switch on her desk and the door unlocked with an audible *click,* then slid open. "Come in, Victor. Let's talk."

"You canceled us." The first words out of his mouth held layers of meaning, but she opted to address the most obvious one.

"I did. I needed a little time before our next session." She gestured to the chair across from her and said firmly, "Sit."

He quirked a brow at her tone and then grinned a little as he eased his big body into a chair that had not been designed with cyborg frames in mind. Normally they met in the larger of the two therapy rooms, sitting on soft couches with carefully programmed scents and music to create an ambiance of welcoming calm.

"You're awfully tiny to be trying to boss me around," he said.

"You came into my sanctuary, pounded on my door, and insisted we have this meeting. I think you've already made enough demands for today, don't you?" It was the hardest line she'd taken with either of them since their first sessions, back when both of them were almost feral with resentment and had no desire to discuss anything except their plans for revenge.

Vic's lips thinned and he nodded slightly. "Point taken. But we really need to talk."

"I know. But I'm not really sure where to begin."

He leaned back in his chair until it creaked in protest. "How about we start with a simple question? What did you do to my brother?"

"That's not a simple question."

"It's still one I need to know the answer to."

"How is he?" she was deflecting, and they both knew it, even though the answer was important to her.

"Moody. Maybe even in mourning for something. I can't really tell." His amber eyes fixed on hers. "But I'm betting you could. You've got some kind of ability to touch other beings' emotions, don't you?"

She nodded, took a deep breath, and gave him the truth. "I'm an empath."

"Shouldn't you disclose that to your patients before you start treating us?"

She flinched at the sharpness to his words. There was distrust there. She didn't blame him, but it still stung.

"If I did that, I wouldn't be allowed to practice." She raised her hands in a gesture that encompassed the room. "I wouldn't even be here. I'd be back on my homeworld with the rest of the *Nazeela Ulo*. By planetary law, we are not permitted to leave unless we are accompanying our masters, and even then, we are not permitted to be gone for long."

He frowned. "Treasure of the people? Is that a literal translation? What does that mean?"

"It means that if I didn't hide my abilities, I'd be little more than a slave."

"So, when you said master…" His expression turned stormy. "Your species has some seriously *fraxxed* up rules."

That made her laugh, relief and amusement bubbling up and easing the tension she'd been holding in. "I think I mentioned that the other night."

"On our date."

"At dinner," she corrected him.

He leaned forward, and this time the chair's squeak of protest was louder. "At a dinner where you sat in my brother's lap and held our hands on the walk home."

"Yes, I did. And then it all went up like a supernova, and here we are." *On the brink of changing everything.* She wasn't ready to admit that last bit out loud. Not yet.

He was quiet for a moment, so close she could smell the subtle mix of soap, the club, and him. "And here we are. Can you tell me what you did to him? I've heard his descriptions, he even shared the footage of what happened from his perspective, but I don't know what he was feeling, and I need to understand."

She fell back into her role as therapist with a feeling close to relief. This was familiar territory. "Why?"

"Because the two people I care about most in the world were involved in something that resulted in one of them shutting down and the other one going into hiding."

It wasn't the answer she'd expected, and for a moment, she didn't know what to say. "I'm sorry."

"For what?"

"Not being there when you both needed me. As your therapist, I should have—"

He was on his feet in a flash, hands planted on her desk as he loomed over her. "We don't need a *fraxxing* therapist, Xori. We need *you*."

She shrank back in her chair, her arms rising into the same gesture of submission she'd used the other night. It was instinctive, and she resented the life that had taught her to react to anger this way. It was part of why she'd chosen this career in the first place. To undo what had been done to herself.

He rounded the desk in a heartbeat, turning her chair and crouching in front of her, his big hands engulfing hers to draw them back down into her lap. "You never have to submit to me, Xori. Never."

"Old habits," she whispered, her throat so tight she could barely force the words out.

"I would never hurt you."

She nodded, swallowed, and tried to find her voice again. "I know. If I didn't believe that, I wouldn't have told you my secret. I wouldn't have..." she smiled a little. "Gone out on what I've been pretending wasn't a date."

"You haven't told me all of it, though." He didn't let go of her hands, and she could feel his emotions pressing into her awareness. Regret. Anger. Affection. Need. So much need it threatened to shatter the last of her resistance. He wanted her, and it forced her to accept how much she wanted him, too.

"Will you tell me what you did the other night. How

did you stop Ward from killing the asshole who hurt you?"

"I took his anger away."

He exhaled softly. "So you *can* do that."

"I can. It's only temporary, though. To do it to someone who carries the rage and pain he does isn't really a kindness."

"Because it doesn't last." Vic's fingers caressed hers. "Show me?"

She managed a tiny shake of her head, knowing it wouldn't deter either of them. It was her last moment of resistance before giving him everything he wanted. She understood now. She'd been waiting for Ward. Until he'd expressed his interest, it had been easy to resist. Now, things were different.

"I have to know." He gave her a small smile. "I need to remember what it was like to be whole and happy."

A sense of trust and longing pushed past her walls, and she stopped trying to block the flow of emotions. "Touch makes all my abilities stronger. I'm trying not to read you right now, but it's difficult when we're connected like this and I don't have your consent."

He tightened his grip on her hands. "It's okay. You have my permission. Read me. Then do what you did for Ward."

"Remember, this won't last." She opened the connection between them, and let it in, the good and the bad. The joy and the sorrow. She held onto the darkness and fed the light back into him, tempering it into something impossibly pure. Later, she'd have to burn off the negative feelings she'd taken from him, but that was part of the price she paid for her gift. Watching Victor's face as all the pain and anger faded away, seeing the peace she brought him, even for a moment, it was a price she was happy to pay.

Ward had been right, it was like walking into sunlight after years in the dark. It was liberating, incredible, and better than any pharma he'd ever taken. There was no guilt or pain. No grief or regret. He'd never believed in a higher power, but if there was such a thing in the vast universe, this was what he thought it would be like to stand in its presence.

"Now you know," Xori whispered. Her voice was strained, and he belatedly realized that whatever she was doing, it came at a cost.

"I know. You can stop."

She nodded, and the aching purity of the moment faded almost immediately as the shadows crept back into his soul. They were heavier now, because he was aware of them again.

"You can do this to anyone?"

"For a little while."

"At what price?"

She tipped her head and smiled at him. "Ah, you figured that out, did you?"

"I've been the universe's chew toy often enough to know that good things always have a cost."

"If it's only for a little while, like what I did for you, it's not bad. Emotion is basically another form of energy, which means it can't be destroyed, only transferred or converted into something else." She touched a talon-tipped nail to her chest. "For now, I've shifted it to me."

He didn't like the idea of her carrying his pain. "What does that mean? Is it hurting you? You should have told me. Dammit, that means you carried Ward's, too. No. Give it back to me."

Her laughter surprised him, but not as much as when she pressed a soft finger to his lips. "Shh. It's alright. I'm not in pain. I can't really explain how it works, there are no words for it in any language."

He took her hand, pressing a kiss to the tip of her finger. "Fix yourself. Now."

"It's not that simple. I need to..." she paused and waved her free hand vaguely in the air between them. "I need to burn off the extra energy is probably the simplest way to describe it."

A wicked little voice started whispering in the back of his mind. "Burn it off, how? Exercise?"

She nodded, but her hand came to rest on her injured knee. "Ideally, yes. That's the fastest way. I'll go for a walk later." She paused. "Maybe you and Ward could come with me?"

"I think I've got a better idea." He stood, then leaned down and brushed his lips against hers in a barely there kiss. He forced himself to hold still, to give her the chance to push him away or tell him no. She didn't.

That was all the permission he needed.

He surged forward, mouth slanting across hers. He

wanted to learn the taste of her lips and explore the curve of her mouth.

She touched his cheek then slid her fingers back to stroke through his hair. Heat streaked through him, the spark of long-repressed desires exploding into a firestorm hotter than the center of a star.

She tugged her hand free from his and twined her arm around his shoulder, her talons drawing tiny lines of fire across the nape of his neck. He ran his hands down her body, memorizing her delicate curves as they flowed beneath his fingers. She was warm, and soft, and the scent of her reminded him of a long-ago mission on a lush, garden world full of flowers that perfumed every breath he took. It had been the closest he'd ever come to experiencing paradise – until today.

"Hold on," he murmured, his words caught in the sweet heat of her mouth. She seemed to understand though, and her hold on him tightened as he straightened up, lifting her into his arms and turning to survey the room.

Her office was spartan, with none of the comfortable furniture or setting of the therapy room he'd been in before. Two mismatched chairs on one side of the cheap, plasti-form desk she used, and slightly less battered chair she'd been sitting in. There was nothing else in the place except for a small table beside a limited-menu food dispenser. Not a lot of options, but he'd find a way.

He eyed the desk again, doing some quick mental math in his head. Good enough. He'd *fraxxing* well *make* it work. He turned and set her down on the edge of the desk, pushing everything on the desktop out of the way without once taking his focus off her.

He placed his hands on her knees, careful not to press down on her injury. He knew her well enough to guess she'd never sought treatment. *If she had medi-bots, this wouldn't be an issue*, part of him mused, while another part, this one louder, pointed out that if he'd been paying *fraxxing* attention, she wouldn't have gotten hurt in the first place.

Guilt filled him. Then Xori unwound one arm and placed her soft hand against his cheek.

"Don't." One word, spoken with such gentleness it broke the cycle of guilt and regret that he'd been about to fall into again.

"But if I'd been faster…"

"Only one being is responsible for what happened to me. The male who struck me because he thought it was his right to do so."

"He was an asshole, but we should have noticed what was happening. That's what we were built to do."

"And I was born to be a tool for males like him, but I'm not. I hid my abilities, learned new skills, and got away from that life. So can you."

He looked down into her lovely face and for one perfect moment he believed her. All the doubts and shadows faded again, only this time it was different. Less, but more. He exhaled and leaned in to kiss her, as if he could somehow hold onto all this if he held on to her.

She moaned. A low, throaty sound that rolled through him and left him hungrier for every part of her.

Her parted lips. Her silken skin. The delicate touch of her tongue as it danced with his, mouths open, hands moving over each other in sensual exploration.

He moved his hand up her thigh, pushing her dress up until there was nothing but bare skin beneath his questing fingers. He eased his hand slowly higher, and she opened her legs to grant him access to the part of her body he needed to explore the most.

"I've wanted you for so long. Why now?" he asked, already hating himself for giving her another chance to change her mind.

"Because I want this too. Even if it isn't smart. I was sitting here trying to decide what to do, what to tell you. To find a way forward for us. Then you were here, banging on my door." She smiled up at him. "I've decided that's a sign from the universe."

"I'll have to send it a thank you note, later." He kissed her again, drinking her in like the finest of wines. When he his hands reached the apex of her thighs, his breath tore out of his lungs in an explosive groan. "You're…. you don't wear…" He stroked a finger over a soft patch of curls that covered her pussy.

"That is one element of your culture I never embraced," she admitted, her cheeks darkening, the delicate stripes growing almost black as she blushed.

"If I had known…" She'd been damned near naked every time they'd had a session. Well, not really, but *damn.*

"Now, you know." She used the same phrase as before, but this time the meaning was vastly different, and he chuckled as he pressed a finger into her slick folds.

She shivered, and a soft sigh escaped her lips as her eyes closed and she let her head fall back. This was what he'd dreamed about. Her submission. Sensual, trusting, complete.

The only element missing was Ward. He should be here, sharing Xori, increasing her pleasure, showing her that the three of them were meant to be together. *Next time.*

He shifted his hand, learning the subtle differences of her body. There weren't many. Her clit was positioned a little differently, but the way she reacted told him it was just as sensitive as a human woman's. Maybe more so.

The thought made his already hard cock strain against the confines of his pants, but he wasn't undoing them. Not this time. This was for her, to help rid her of the emotional baggage she'd taken from him.

He moved further between her legs and slid a finger into her entrance, slow and gentle, and was rewarded with another moan. Her delicate talons glided over the fabric of his shirt, and he wished he'd thought to take it off before they'd gotten started. He wanted to feel her hands on him, but there wasn't anything short of an explosion that would make him let go of her. Not until she'd come for him.

She rocked her hips against his fingers, her kisses more urgent now, her soft sounds of pleasure offering a guide to what she liked best. She coiled her uninjured leg around his thigh, pulling him in closer. Her hands tightened on his shoulders and she levered herself off the table, grinding herself against him, her eyes locked on his, their silver depths gleaming like moonlight on deep water.

"Come for me, blossom."

"Victor…" his name came out as a gasp as he pressed his thumb against the fluttering pulse at the center of her clit.

She came hard, her soft voice rising into a shuddering cry of pleasure, It was accompanied by a tearing sound and the fiery burn of her talons scoring the skin of his shoulders. His cock throbbed, aching to be buried inside her, but he didn't move. He simply held her as she shivered and bucked in his arms, reveling in the fact that she was letting him witness this private moment, and that he'd carry her marks on his back for a little while. His nanotech would heal him sooner than he'd like. But for now, she'd marked him as hers.

She stirred and uttered a delicate sigh, and he smiled down at her. "You are so beautiful you take my breath away."

"You did a few things that took mine, too." She blushed again, her body still shivering with the aftershocks of her orgasm.

He withdrew his hand from her, his fingers slick with her essence. He licked it from his fingers, his eyes never leaving hers. She tasted sweet, and again he was reminded of his time on the garden planet they'd visited once. Flowers and sun-ripened fruit. Paradise.

She made a tiny squeaking sound and dropped her gaze.

"Don't you dare be embarrassed, blossom. You're glorious, and delicious, and I cannot wait until I can taste you again."

"Again? We're not supposed to be doing this at all. Human rules are quite clear about that."

"Again." He repeated, letting a note of command slip into his tone. "And before you quote the rules at me, let me remind you of something. None of us are *human*. Not you, not me. Not Ward."

"But you're…"

He stopped her words with a kiss. "We're cyborgs. Ever since I've been freed, I've tried to be human, and it hasn't worked out for me. I don't need to be human to be happy." The words exploded like grenades inside his head, tearing through walls he didn't know existed.

She beamed, laughing. "Did you just have a breakthrough after giving me the best orgasm of my life?"

"Uh. Yes?" Then he caught up to what she'd said and grinned. "Best of your life, huh?"

"That's not the part of my question you should be focusing on right now." She tried to smooth her dress back over her bare thighs, but he was still too close for that to work.

He took her hands in his and squeezed. "See, this is what I meant before. It's not your therapy that's fixing us. It's you."

She nodded, and he saw acceptance in her

expression. "Then I suppose we won't need to reschedule you and Ward for anymore sessions."

"Nope. No more appointments with you. From now on, we're going out on dates."

Her face lit up in a smile brighter than a hundred suns. "Yes."

He kissed her again, gentle this time. "And did we burn off that negative energy you took from me?"

She was quiet for a moment, then nodded. "We did." Her lips quirked, and she laughed again. "I never considered… I think, maybe, I know how to help you both, and then you return the favor."

A rush hit him, euphoric, hopeful, and full of wicked images of just how the three of them could burn off whatever darkness she lifted from their hearts. "Hell, yes."

CHAPTER FIVE

WARD DOWNED his drink in one shot, letting the alcohol burn its way down to his belly. It had been a long shift at the tables. There was a new scam making the rounds, and he'd caught three fools trying it out at his starburst table. They'd all been thrown out and barred from ever returning. Then there'd been a fight between two idiots who thought the other was cheating, when the truth was they were both just lousy players with worse luck. That little incident had required a call to Corp-Sec and a pile of paperwork.

He'd been in a crap mood by the time he was off the clock, and then he'd learned that while he was stuck working, his *fraxxing* twin had been scoring with Xori. He should be happy about that. It was all part of his plan. But there was a burn in his gut that had nothing to do with the booze.

He slammed the empty glass down on the table and

picked up the shot next to it in one fluid motion, tossing it back as fast as the first one.

"I thought you'd be pleased. She's agreed to go out with us. Be with us. This is good news." Vic was seated across from him in the back of the VIP area, looking more than a little confused. *Join the club.* He wasn't sure what the hell was going on with him, either.

"Yeah. It is. I just…" Ward set the glass in his hand down with more care this time and tried to smile. He suspected it came out as more than a grimace.

"Wait. Are you jealous?" Vic's eyes widened. "Holy *fraxx*. You are!"

He grunted as he chewed that thought over for a moment. *Shit.* That's what it was.

"Maybe."

"Idiot."

"Asshole."

"The plan is to make her ours, Wolf. Not mine. Not yours. Ours."

"I hear what you're saying." He also heard the edge in his words and made a real effort to dial it back. Since Xori had reminded him what it felt like to be normal, he'd fought to get back there on his own. He'd been in the dark so long he'd forgotten how to feel any other way, and finding the path without her wasn't easy. But if he could manage just a little more, maybe that would be enough to push Vic back into the light for good.

He eyed the third shot he'd ordered, but left it on the table for now. "So, she can fix us, but it won't last, and in order to do it she has to take our messed-up energy into herself."

"Yeah. Not thrilled about that part."

"Me either."

"But I have to say I'm a fan of the solution." Vic shot him a shit-eating grin that stunned him. He hadn't seen his brother smile like that in… *fraxx*. Way too damned long.

"I bet." He tried to grin back, and this time it felt almost natural.

"Next time, it will be all three of us, together."

"Yeah, but where?" He waved a hand around the bustling club. "It's not like we've got a lot of options. Our room is barely big enough for two of us, and I have no intention of letting this pack of lunatics have a ringside seat to our love life."

Vic groaned. "*Fraxx*, no. This is technically our first date. I'm pretty sure it's bad form to ask if she'd take us home with her already."

"There needs to be a dating manual," Ward agreed.

They sat in silence for a few minutes, both of them considering their options. He was about to suggest they give in and ask their batch-siblings for a little help when a familiar voice called out to them.

"A wolf and a fox walked into a bar… Damn. One day, I'm going to have to learn the punchline to that joke." Royan Watson strolled up to their table, several others following up behind. "Hey, you two. What's with the dour looks? You're both glowering at your meals like they owe you scrip."

Royan, semi-reformed bad boy and a member of the Nova Club's cadre of rebels, had a few days of stubble on his cheeks that he somehow made work with the suit he wore, which probably cost more than he and Vic earned in a year.

"I still don't get it," Ward gestured for him and the others to join their table. "How the hell did you, a scruffy freighter jockey from the ass-end of nowhere, wind up married to one of our corporate overlords?"

"Charm. Sex appeal…"

"And a *fraxxing* ton of good luck," Owen added, giving his husband an affectionate swat to the back of his head. "He always glosses over that part. But luck is the only way I can explain why Tianna ever agreed to marry the likes of us."

"Denz? What the hell are you doing back here? I thought we'd lost you to the glamor of colony life." Vic greeted the big half-Torski lurking behind the others. Colony life seemed to suit him. He was tanned, relaxed, and sporting a new beard as coal black as his hair.

The male shrugged. "Chance's departure and subsequent change in employment meant making some changes to the colony's agreement with the corporations. Someone on the governing council needed to hammer out the details, and I drew the short straw. I decided it was easier to come here and do it face-to-face."

Ward suspected that was only part of the truth. Denz had lost family to another of the Gray Men's involuntary cyborg assassins not so long ago, and the killer's clone had recently been sent to live in Haven, the new colony that was home to Vardarians, humans, and the last cyborgs to be freed from the Gray's control. Shadow had nothing to do with Zale's death, but seeing the face of the woman who'd killed your closest kin every day would be enough to make anyone want to leave the planet.

"Seems like a good time to do it," Vic said. "What with half the corporations already sending their advance teams here before the big party."

"Exactly. Plus, I missed this place. The vat-grown food, the stink of recycled air…" Denz drew in a deep breath and grinned broadly enough his fangs showed. "Also, a decent ale. Those Vardarians are wizards with technology, but their liquor leaves a lot to be desired."

They all laughed, and the group fell into an easy flow of conversation. Ward didn't say more than a few words. It was easier for him to stay on the fringes of groups like this one, even when they were all his friends.

Eventually, the topic shifted back to them. "So, what have you two been up to?"

"Not much. Work, mostly."

"And getting to know our new batch-sister," Vic added.

"How's Chance doing? Settling in?" Denz asked, his expression earnest. It was clear that checking up on his escaped cyborg was another reason he'd left the colony.

"Apart from the fact Erik doesn't want to let her out of his sight, yet? Yeah. We're all taking turns teaching her some hand-to-hand skills. The next asshole who tries take her away from us is going to get his head handed to him." Vic said with a hint of pride.

Ward still carried a lot of guilt about the way he'd treated Chance. He'd thought she was a threat to his family and reacted as such, never giving her the benefit of the doubt. He'd been ready to send her back without hearing her side. If that had happened, he'd never have known she was family, too.

"I'm glad. She was struggling in the colony. Her fear of open spaces made her life hellish." Denz shook his head. "She's not the only one fighting that demon, but hers was the worst case."

"You have a therapist for them?" Ward asked.

"Not yet. I was going to talk to Dr. Virness."

His hackles went up. "She's not moving to Liberty. She's ours."

They all stopped and stared at him.

"Whoa. Did I hear what I think I heard?" Royan smirked.

"That was definitely jealousy, with a couple of crates of possessiveness on the side." Owen nodded.

"I was just going to see if she could recommend anyone." Denz had his hands raised in surrender.

"So," Royan drawled. "Care to spill? Or do I need to go ask Cyn and Zura what the scoop is?"

Vic swore and Ward groaned before saying, "Do not get our sisters involved. Yours is terrifyingly astute, and our sister-in-law is flat out terrifying."

"Truth." Owen agreed. "Best you tell us yourselves."

"That's blackmail," Ward grumbled.

"In my former line of work, we called it incentive," Owen replied.

He looked at his brother. "We're being threatened by a playboy and a pirate. This is our life now?"

Vic looked around the merry group and then grinned at him. "I'm surprisingly okay with it."

Something shifted deep in his chest with a pang that made him want to wince. Vic was healing. Ward had thought that before, but this time he was sure of it. Vic had begun drifting into a new orbit, a new life. That meant that soon, he'd be moving on, and Ward would be alone in the dark. This was what he wanted, but now that it was happening, it hurt more than he'd expected.

"If you're done with the commentary, we're still waiting for an explanation," Royan said.

"Yeah, yeah. Cool your boosters. There's not much to tell. We finally got her to agree to go out for dinner with us the other night," Vic said.

"It went great, but on the way home, some asshole Pheran took offense to someone of her status daring to breathe the same air as he and kicked her." Ward finished.

"*Fraxx* that. Who? Did you kick his ass?" Royan said.

"Damned near," Ward admitted, careful not to give too much away. "But in the end Xori managed to convince me that discretion was the better part of not getting arrested."

"So, you two want a nice, safe place to take her on your next date?" Owen said, giving his husband a meaningful glance that made no sense to Ward. Was that what it was like for other non-cyborgs when he and Vic started communicating via their internal channel? It was damned annoying.

"Got any suggestions?" Vic asked.

Royan nodded to Owen. "Actually, yeah. We know the perfect place."

"Where? And keep in mind we're not married to one of the richest women in the galaxy," Ward said.

"As it happens, there's a shiny new ship docked at the station right now. Now, I'm not handing over the keys so you can take her for a joy ride, but so long as you two ruffians promise to leave her parked, she's yours."

"New ship? Tianna's? The one that costs more scrip than a small planet?"

Owen laughed. "That's the one. The Faerie Queene is more luxurious than anything you'll find on the station, and the food is exceptional. You won't even know it came out of the dispensers."

"It's fully automated, too. Bots and droids of every description, so you won't need to lift a finger." Royan winked. "At least not when it comes to dinner and clean up. The rest is up to the two of you."

"We don't need help from a *fraxxing* droid, thank you." Ward glowered and downed his last shot of booze.

"Using your ship for a date is one thing, but..." Vic trailed off.

"The Queene is bigger than some hotels out here. We'll assign you guest quarters. You forget, we've lived in the Nova's rooms. Not exactly romantic," Owen said.

"And very small beds," Royan chimed in.

"All your human furnishings are tiny," Denz muttered. "That's one thing I miss about Haven. My huge, custom-built bed."

Everyone laughed, but Vic leaned forward, eyes bright. "That reminds me. If you're looking for a little taste of home, you should check out the *Dobnar Brin*. A Torski family run it. Amazing food."

"Best ale on the station, too. Just don't tell Kit and Luke I said that." Ward said.

Denz nodded. "Thanks."

They kept talking, but Ward retreated to the fringes of the conversation again, letting the words swirl around him without taking part. His thoughts were consumed with images of Xori and what might happen when they were together again. When he'd decided it was time to bring Xori and Vic together, he'd made one miscalculation: he hadn't realized how much he'd want her, too. But wanting her didn't mean he deserved her. He drummed his fingers against his thigh and went through the litany of reasons he couldn't have her. It was a long list, but he had to go through it several times before it truly sank in that a future with her could never be more than wishes and fairy dust. It wouldn't, couldn't last. Not for a broken killer like him.

Xori walked into her quarters and headed straight for the food dispenser. She ordered a glass of cold water and two tablets of pain-blocker. She'd just had an intense session with an IAF soldier suffering from PTSD, and her heart ached almost as much as her knee right now. He'd lost more than half his team in a shuttle crash, but somehow, he'd walked away with only a few minor bruises. The physical damage had healed. The wounds to his psyche would take longer, and the scars of his loss would be with him the rest of his life.

She wished there was more she could do for her patients, especially the ones still so deep in their pain that they couldn't see past it. It clouded their thinking and obscured their view of the future. These were the times she was tempted to use her gift the most, to show those in her care what life could be like after the hurt faded, but she couldn't. Not only because she needed to keep it a secret to protect herself, but for their sakes, too. Her gift was a double-edged blade. It took the pain away, but it couldn't keep it at bay for long. Back home, the *Nazeela Ulo* were little more than slaves, kept by the powerful to provide peace and a pain-free existence to their masters, who quickly grew addicted to a life without emotional upset of any kind. It was a nightmarish life for the *m'bara*, one she'd trained long and hard to be able to escape.

She sank down on her simple couch, a standard model that she'd seen throughout the station. Comfortable. Plain. Inexpensive. This one was a light gray color that matched the décor of her quarters, and she made a mental note to find something to brighten the place up. A cushion maybe, or a blanket. Anything to offset the sea of neutrality she lived in.

Home had been full of vibrant colors. They were too poor to afford much in the way of furnishings, but what little they had was a brilliant array of mismatched fabrics, and their tiny yard had almost as many flowers as it had the fruits and vegetables they grew to supplement their meager diet.

She'd spent hours out in that garden, practicing the mental exercises that would allow her to control her talents, if they ever manifested. Sometimes they skipped a generation. Her mother had only the mildest of ability, and she'd hoped that her daughter would be the same. It hadn't turned out that way.

When Xori had come into her gifts near the start of her second decade, she had rapidly eclipsed her mother's skill. She'd grown stronger every day, and every evening they'd practiced relentlessly to ensure that when the time of testing came, she could hide her gift.

It was the only test she'd ever been happy to fail.

Even then, she'd had to be careful. The slightest slip could ruin everything she'd worked for. She'd worked any job she could find, pushing herself to her breaking point more than once to earn enough money to pay for her education. She'd struggled to find a balance between work and school until a few years into her training when her high marks qualified her for financial support. She'd still worked, though, saving everything she could against the day she could book transport off- world.

She rubbed her eyes, making spots dance behind her lids. *Why am I dwelling on the past?* She hadn't thought about it in years. It was decades since she'd left Phera Prime, and her parents, behind.

The answer wasn't difficult to determine. The confrontation the other night had stirred up memories of her old life. Then there was her decision to reveal her gift to Vic. She'd given him the power to send her back to Phera Prime and the existence she'd fought so hard to escape. Not that she regretted it. She trusted Vic and Ward not to tell anyone. But she couldn't help but feel vulnerable.

She started to walk around her quarters, a task made easier now the pain-blocker was starting to work. Was going out with them again the right thing to do? Even now she'd agreed to a date, she was having reservations. What would the IAF think about her decision? She might not be human, but the IAF was, and like most military organizations, it was bound by a vast array of rules and regulations.

She paced some more, her thoughts zipping around in ever-tightening circle like a ship in a failing orbit. Anxiety crept in, making her walk faster.

It wasn't until her knee twinged again that she realized what she was doing and made herself stop.

"What's wrong with me?" she asked the empty walls.

She walked gingerly over to the couch and sat down again, setting her hands on her knees and closing her eyes. After a few minutes of controlled breathing, clarity returned, and with it came the answer.

"I'm a *vething* idiot." She told her patients to look beyond the obvious, to question if what you think you're worried about is really the problem, or if it's just a diversion. Nova Force's reaction to her burgeoning relationship was the distraction.

She huffed out a breath. The real issue had nothing

to do with Vic or Ward. It was far simpler. She didn't feel safe. That arrogant *gurani* Pheran male had torn away her sense of security. Made her vulnerable and afraid.

The next second she was on her feet and headed for the door. She wouldn't let him do that to her. If she were one of her patients, she'd encourage them to acknowledge the fear and then face it. It was time to take her own advice.

She was already halfway to the checkpoint before she realized she wasn't wearing her *matyri*. She'd never been out onto the main station without it before. It was a ritual she'd maintained no matter where she lived. An echo of her past.

One it was time she let go of. She tightened her fingers into a fist and kept walking.

She hadn't gone out much since the attack. In fact, apart from visiting the Nova for a sim-pod session with Nyx, she only went to her office. She'd let her world get smaller and hadn't even noticed.

The slight burn of her anger made it a little easier to walk into the bustle and hum of the main concourse. Her heart was beating too fast, and she had to stop herself from turning every few steps to check behind her. She didn't want to run into that *taryn-nah* bully again.

She had no destination in mind when she started out, but before long, she found herself walking with purpose. Her stomach had decided to follow the scent of food. The promenade opened into an intersection with banks of mag-levs on one side and a bullet train platform on the other. Vendors filled the rest of the space, selling food, drinks, and trinkets to the ever-changing throng as they moved along the promenade.

She wove through the crowd carefully, still hyper-aware of everyone around her at all times. Every time she caught sight of the color blue she tensed, and by the time she made her way to the stall she wanted, she felt weary and wrung out.

Atun and Ma'ti were there, as always, preparing their usual assortment of Pheran street food. She exchanged pleasantries with them, trying to ignore the fact that Ma'ti stared at her ear several times as they chatted, touching her own more than once.

Xori pretended not to notice. It was odd not having the familiar weight of her *matyri*, but it was freeing, too.

"You hear there is a Pheran trade delegation on the station?" Atun asked as he handed her a cup of *jazza* berry juice.

"No. I've been holed up in my office the last few days. I'm not surprised, though. There will be representatives from every species and planet here in the next few weeks. And I had a run in with an unpleasant higher caste male a few days ago."

Ma'ti made a soft noise of distress. "We heard. His name is Yvern Tesk, one of the *taryn-nah* caste. Some of his staff came by. It was like being home again, and not in a good way."

"What did they do?"

Atun cocked his head and dipped his shoulder low. "What they always do. Took what they wanted and offered only insults for payment."

He handed her a carefully wrapped packet of *shecka*, the bread still warm from the oven and rich with the scent of grilled meat.

"Did you tell anyone?" Her question came out in hushed, careful tones.

"No. Would only make things worse. You know how it is."

She nodded. "I do."

She tapped a few keys on her comm unit, paying for her meal and adding a little extra.

Atun checked the payment info, and scowled at her. "Too much."

She smiled at him. "My finger slipped."

Her mood buoyed up for the moment, she picked her way through the crowd, scanning the edges for a free space where she could eat. After a few minutes, the sense of unease returned again. She ignored it. It was because they'd talked about the Pheran trade delegation. That was all.

Someone touched her shoulder, and she nearly jumped out of her stripes.

"Xori? Oh my stars, I'm sorry! I didn't mean to startle you."

"Chance?" She smiled up at the cyborg female and her mate, Erik. "Hello, you two."

"Hey," the blonde man with Chance smiled down at her. "You okay?"

"Just finding the crowd a bit overwhelming today."

"I know the feeling." Chance pointed to a vacant table not far away. "Want to sit for a bit? We're here for a bite to eat, and then we're going up to the observation deck to see if I'm ready to look at some real stars instead of the ones in the sim-pod."

"Good for you!" They moved to the table and every other interested party drifted away from the newly claimed spot the moment they spotted Erik. He'd been a cage fighter at the Nova until recently, and he carried himself with the same air of danger she'd sensed from Ward and Victor.

She and Chance chatted while Erik went in search of food, and the unsettled feeling faded again. She ate as Chance shared snippets of her new job and how much she was enjoying her new life on the station.

It struck Xori that Chance had risked everything to come out to the Drift looking for a better life, and she'd found it. It was a good reminder. Life was about taking risks. She'd taken big ones to get this far, but lately, she'd been playing things safe. It was time for that to change.

CHAPTER SIX

Vic stepped out of the rear of the transport Tianna had provided for tonight and opened Xori's door for her before the driver could do more than unfasten his harness. He offered his hand, and she took it, rising from her seat to stand in front of him. She was a vision, her hair piled up in some sort of elaborate do that he knew Ward was itching to disassemble, and her dress was a simple sheath of brilliant silver that showed off her slender shape to perfection.

Ward joined them, his eyes locked on Xori. "I know I mentioned this already, but you look stunning. You shine brighter than any star out there." He waved toward the viewports that lined the docking area.

Vic hadn't been to this part of the station since Tianna had taken over her father's company and made Astek her new base of operations. This entire section was now the exclusive territory of Astek Corporation.

Royan had arranged everything, including putting

their handprints on file as official guests. He'd also ensured no other Pherans had access to this area at the moment. So there'd be no risk of more unpleasantness from that quarter. Security was tight. They'd been required to prove their identities at two automated security checkpoints to get this far, and there wasn't another living being in sight beside their driver.

"You did mention it, but I'm happy to hear it again." Xori was smiling as she looked around in curiosity. "This whole section is just for Tianna and her business?"

"One of the many perks of being the boss," Vic said.

It was a short walk to the docking hatch, and he noted with amusement that the carpet here was so thick he couldn't hear the slightest noise from their footfalls as they walked over it.

"I'm almost afraid to touch anything," Ward muttered as they approached.

"Me too," Xori whispered. "Do we have a plan if an alarm goes off?"

"Sure. You and I run for it, and we leave Vic to take the blame. Sound good?"

She laughed. "Not really. I am not running far in these shoes." She lifted the hem of her dress to show off footwear that had about as much substance as a soap bubble. "Plus, I agreed to go out on a date with both of you, so you can't ditch Vic before the evening even begins."

Vic halted mid-stride and pivoted to face her, his next words coming as a surprise to everyone, including himself. "If anything ever happens. Alarms, explosions, or someone so much as makes you feel threatened, you go with Ward. He'll take care of you." His eyes snapped to his twin. "Won't you, Wolf?"

Ward's fist thumped his chest in a salute. He grimaced, turning the salute into an obscene gesture. "Asshole. You know I hate it when you pull rank on me."

"Was that an automatic reaction?" Xori was watching them both, her eyes bright with curiosity.

"Yeah. We're a command team, same as Kit and Luke. The rest of our batch were programmed to follow our orders, but I'm hard-coded to follow his." Ward jerked his thumb at Vic.

"You expecting trouble?" Ward asked through their link.

"No. Don't know why I said that. But if anything happens…"

"I'll make sure she's safe. Always."

"Good," Vic replied.

Ward surprised him by adding. *"If your gut starts telling you there's trouble coming,* fraxxing *say something this time."*

He flinched, and Xori caught it. "What? What did I miss?" she asked.

Ward cursed under her breath. "Sorry. That was a cheap shot."

He waved it off. "Maybe, but that doesn't make it less true."

Xori folded her arms across her chest and muttered something in Pheran so fast he only caught every second or third word.

"Uh… did she just threaten to paint our heads with honey?" Ward asked, as confused as he was.

"I thought she said something about redecorating our faces," Vic said.

She glared up at them, though her lips were quirked up in a hint of a smile. "I said that if you two don't start explaining yourselves, I'll ask Cyn to tear your heads off so I can use them to decorate my office."

Ward croaked with strangled laughter. "Well, clearly you've been spending too much time at the Nova. Our sister-in-law is rubbing off on you in alarming ways."

"She's fascinating."

"She's a lunatic. Who else would take on our batch-brothers?" Vic said, then walked the last few steps to the access panel. He placed his hand on the scanner and the door slid open. "Dinner awaits."

Xori shook her head and settled back on her heels. "Oh no. Not until you explain what happened a moment ago."

It took him a second to rewind the conversation to remember what she meant. The recollection made him wince, again. "Not out here, please."

Her expression softened immediately. "Alright."

"Thank you." It was one of the many facets of her personality he enjoyed. She could be relentless and stubborn during their sessions, forcing them to face truths they'd rather avoid at all costs, but she was never confrontational. His gaze slid to Ward. Unlike others he knew, she would never pick a fight just because they wanted someone to yell at.

Walking onto the ship was like stepping into

another world. The air was crisp and clean and carried a subtle scent that reminded him of green, growing things despite the fact there wasn't a single plant in view. The decks were covered in a thick, red carpet, and the walls had actually been textured and painted to hide the steel beneath.

A hologram shimmered into existence in front of them. It was a small female figure about two feet high, with blonde hair, slender limbs, and translucent wings growing out of her back. "Welcome aboard the *Faerie Queene*. My name is Tink, and I'm the ship's AI. If you follow me, I will guide you to your suite for the evening."

They stared at each other. An AI with its own hologram that could just flit about the ship?

"I think I need to start charging Tianna more for our sessions," Xori whispered.

"Indeed, you should. Your current rate is twenty-two percent less than standard, Dr. Virness," the AI replied, then tipped her head slightly. "And you have been a great help to my owner. Thank you for that."

"You're very welcome, Tink."

They followed the hologram along a spacious hallway and into an elevator that let them out several floors down. All three of them were silent, drinking in the opulence that saturated every detail. It wasn't overdone, exactly. It was simply wealth on a scale that none of them had ever experienced before.

Despite all Royan's reassurances, they kept Xori between them, some instinct making them both aware of the need to keep her safe, even here. He didn't question it. He'd made that mistake once, and the cost had been steep.

Tink led them to an open door. "This is your suite. All the housekeeping bots have been programmed to respond to your requests, and I can be summoned simply by calling my name."

"Do you have a privacy mode?" Vic asked.

"Of course. It's already been enabled. I have a subroutine that monitors for mentions of my name, but nothing else. Will this suffice?"

"It will. Thank you."

"You are welcome, Victor. I shall leave you to enjoy your evening." Tink didn't simply blink out of existence, she flew into the nearest wall and vanished into a cloud of sparkles that lingered for a few minutes before fading away.

Xori giggled. "Interesting exit."

"What I want to know is how it could tell us apart. Not many can," Ward wandered further into the room as he talked, looking around in wide-eyed amazement.

Xori laughed harder. "It isn't difficult."

They spun to stare at her. "Care to share the secret?"

She waved a hand. "Nope. You still owe me an explanation for what happened outside."

"Right." He really didn't want to talk about it. It was one of the few things they hadn't mentioned to her in their sessions.

"Wine?" Ward cut in. He'd pulled a bottle – an actual, old-world style *glass* bottle – out of an ice bucket and held it up.

"Good thinking." Vic pulled out a chair for Xori and

the three of them took their places. Like everything else, the chairs were lush, comfortable, and decorated in shades of red and gold. There were menus on the table, and a tablet that would send their orders to the galley to be prepared and delivered by the household bots. It was the perfect setting for their first official date. Now all they had to do was convince Xori they were a risk worth taking.

Ward poured the wine without reading the label. He knew more about astrophysics than he did about wine making, but he was confident that if it was stocked on *this* ship, it would be incredible.

"To new beginnings," Xori raised her glass as he finished pouring.

They answered her toast and drank, then Vic leaned forward. "I'll tell you what Wolf and I were talking about out in the corridor, but once I do, I'm hoping we can forget about it and just enjoy our evening. This isn't the time or place to go over it in detail."

She nodded. "Another time. Maybe in my office? That would make it sort of official, instead of just the three of us being together. Even though we're not doing sessions anymore, I still want to help you."

"Setting up a few boundaries?" Vic asked.

She flashed them a little smile. "A few, yes. Probably not enough to keep everyone happy, but well…as you said. Human rules really don't apply to me."

"Or us," Ward agreed.

"Alright then." Vic said, his voice shifting to a story-telling cadence. "The night we got taken, I had a bad feeling. A gut instinct about Ariel. I dismissed it without saying anything. Ward made a crack about it. Said this time, if I sensed a problem, to say something."

"I was out of line," Ward said. They'd both made mistakes, and tonight really wasn't the moment to discuss it. He didn't want to talk about this at all, which is why they'd never brought it up in their sessions, but things were different now. She needed to know.

Ward rubbed the back of his neck, trying to ease the tension there. "When it was happening, I didn't see it." He managed to keep most of the anger and regret out of his voice. "Not at the time. Later it was obvious she was setting us up."

"If I'd said something, I could have stopped it," Vic said.

"If I had been thinking with my big brain instead of my little one, I might have seen it." He wanted to take the words back the second they flew out of his mouth. It's not that Xori didn't know they'd been ordered to fuck Ariel once they were under her control. They'd covered that early on, though thankfully not in detail. The thing was, neither of them had ever mentioned that sex was how she'd caught them in the first place.

Sitting here, on their first official date, seemed like a spectacularly bad time to mention it.

Xori blew out a soft breath, then nodded to herself and stood. "Since this isn't a formal session, I have something I need to say to you both."

That can't be good. He looked over at Vic, who was giving him a slightly panicked look in return.

"Xori, before you say any—" she raised her hand and he stopped talking. He'd said more than enough already.

"You both feel like you failed yourselves, and each other." She looked at them, her eyes mild. "You're both *fraxxing* idiots. Stop blaming yourself for what happened. Blame that bitch Ariel, instead."

Her statement hit like a hammer, driving home a point she'd tried to make more than once in far gentler terms. This time, he heard her. He was on his feet and had her in his arms as fast as he could move. There'd been no thought process other than the need to hold her and tell her how amazing she was. "You…" was all he managed to say before his mouth crashed down on hers, and words didn't matter anymore.

She kissed him back, rising on her toes, her hands tangling in his hair as she tugged him closer. His cock hardened so fast it was almost painful, and when she moaned his name against his lips, he dropped a hand to her ass and hauled her in tight against his body so she could feel how she affected him. He needed her to understand, because there was no one else in this starsforsaken universe that could make him this crazy. He didn't deserve her. He certainly couldn't keep her. But tonight, he was going to have her so he wouldn't have to walk back into the darkness without at least one memory to hold on to.

~

She'd known how tonight would end. At least, how she'd hoped it would. The three of them together in ways she'd only dreamed about. She could feel their tension, the crackle of anticipation, and the low thrum of desire that buzzed around them both. She sensed darker things, too, mixed up with the need and sudden madness that seemed to have infected them all.

Vic stepped in behind her, his hands moving across her shoulders, then along her flanks to rest on her hips, Ward started undoing her hair, gently teasing it loose from the magnetic clasp holding it in place. She'd done it on purpose, knowing Ward would want to undo it the way he'd threatened to so many times in their sessions.

He drew her hair over her shoulder, lifting a handful to his lips, and then rubbing it across his cheek.

Behind her, Vic dusted kisses soft as snowflakes over the newly bared skin at the nape of her neck.

"Tell us what you need, little star, and we'll make it happen." Ward coiled a strand of her hair around his finger, using it to draw her in for another scorching kiss.

These huge, dangerous males had her caught between them, and it was the most intoxicating feeling in the world. Their bodies were hard, and she could feel their cocks pressing into her like twin steel bars, but their touch was gentle and their kisses made her feel like she could fly. An idea kindled in the back of her brain. "Tink. Can you lower the gravity in here, enough we can float but still have some control?"

There was a brief pause before the AI answered. "I can. I will need to secure all furnishings and extend containment fields over loose objects. Do you wish me to proceed?"

"Yes."

"Proceeding. Gravity will change in five seconds. Five-four-three-two-one." There was a single, unified *clunk* as the magnetic clamps on every piece of furniture activated at once. Her stomach did the familiar drop and flutter that happened every time she'd been in micro-gravity.

"Interesting idea," Vic murmured, his voice rich with amusement and arousal.

"You are full of surprises, little star of mine," Ward kissed her softly, then looked over at his brother. "Up?"

"And over," Vic agreed.

Before she could ask what they meant by over, Ward pushed off and they rose into the air, spinning slowly. Xori had to lock her gaze on the viewport to give her mind something to focus on while the rest of her struggled to come to terms with the loss of up and down.

It didn't seem to bother Ward or Victor, but they'd been created with an awareness of how to function in all sorts of environments, including Zero-G.

The spinning slowed, then stopped, leaving them floating prone in an open area of their suite while keeping the same basic orientation as before. Ceiling up, floor down. The subtle tug of gravity reasserted itself, a barely-there sensation that meant they'd slowly drift back toward the floor over time. Vic was beneath her now, Ward above her.

He released her, taking off his shirt and letting it

float away before taking her into his arms again and kissing her like it was his last night of life. She knew the feeling. There was something about tonight that was special, a subtle shimmer of near-magic that couldn't last. It was a night for making memories.

She let her hands drift over his bare skin, exploring as much of him as she could reach, her mouth still mated to his.

Vic released her, and she felt the loss of his warmth against her back even though the room wasn't cold. When he returned, he undid the fastenings on the back of her dress, following the curve of her spine with one calloused finger.

She eased her arms out of the dress one at a time, and both men groaned even as Ward pulled it down toward her feet, baring her body to them for the first time.

"I've imagined this so many times," Vic whispered, his lips tracing the stripes that marked her skin.

She shivered, then gasped as Ward tugged her dress down her legs and sent it drifting off to join the rest of their clothes.

"You're beautiful." He murmured, cupping her breasts in his hands, his thumbs stroking over her nipples until they were tight nubs that tingled with every touch.

"*Fraxx*, I don't know what I want to do more. Kiss you, play with these or…." He let his hand drift lower, brushing over the soft skin of her stomach.

"Make her come for us, Wolf." There was just

enough command in Vic's words to make her quiver, her pussy creaming at the implication of his words.

"Best order you've ever given me." Ward's mouth slanted across hers with a fire that could rival a star, the force of it enough to send them into another slow spin.

Both of them released her, leaving her to rotate on her own for a moment, then they were back, two bare-chested gods with identical smiles that held more than a little of their predatory nature. She was more than happy to be the prey they hunted.

"I really like this no panties thing," Ward told her as he positioned at her feet, his hands on her ankles, coaxing her legs apart with gentle pressure.

"It's going to make it *fraxxing* hard to behave when we're in public," Vic said.

She laughed. "I'll wear some if it worries you so much. Then you won't be distracted."

"Nope. Bad idea. Forget I said anything." Vic drifted into her line of vision, closing in for a kiss of his own in a move that wouldn't have been possible in normal gravity.

She lost herself in the heat of it, arched and gasped as Ward's fingers slid into the wet folds of her sex. Her world exploded into a host of sensations too myriad to keep track of. Vic's mouth on hers, his hands on her breasts, stroking and kneading, capturing her moans against his lips and tongue.

Ward worked her clit with deft, intimate touches that had her bucking and writhing in seconds, her actions sending them spinning again. He slipped a finger inside her, then two, fucking her with one hand, the other wrapped around her thigh to anchor them together.

She rode his fingers until she was near the edge of her control, the pleasure almost more than she could bear.

Vic pulled away, his amber gaze bright with desire. "He's going to make you come soon, isn't he?"

She gave a tiny nod, not trusting herself to speak. If she said anything, it would be to beg them to fuck her, to stop playing and take her hard, the way she'd imagined it in her dreams.

"Not yet. Not until I've tasted her." Ward withdrew his hand.

"Don't stop," the words tumbled out of her mouth.

"Stop? *Fraxx* no. Not for hours yet. But now we've got you to ourselves, there's a list of things we want to do to you, and with you," Vic said.

"Me, too," she admitted.

"I'm going to want to hear that list, right after I hear you come." Vic dropped his head to suckle one nipple into the heat of his mouth just as Ward's tongue ran along the seam of her pussy's lips. She jerked at the twin explosions of pleasure, arching herself into their touch. Ward's fingers parted her folds, exposing her to him. Then his mouth was on her flesh, his tongue flicking across her swollen nub until she could hardly breathe.

Ward gripped her hips and latched onto her clit, sucking at her flesh as he hummed a sharp note that sent her spinning out of control. She came hard, her soft gasps the only sound in the room as she bucked against his mouth. He didn't let up, drawing out her release and leaving her adrift in a sea of blissful, breathless pleasure.

She barely noticed when one of them gathered her into his arms. "Tink, return to normal gravity please. Slowly. No countdown."

"Confirmed." The AI replied, and a few seconds later their flight came to an end, leaving her snuggled in Victor's embrace.

"I hope you're not hungry right now, because dinner isn't on my immediate agenda," he said, already carrying her toward the largest of the bedrooms they'd seen.

"Food can wait. All I need is you." She looked until she spotted Ward standing a few paces away, then held out her hand to him. "Both of you."

CHAPTER SEVEN

ONE OF THESE DAYS, Vic would figure out how to stay in control when he was around Xori.

It wouldn't be today. He'd held back for too long to want to rein his desires in anymore. Ward felt the same loss of control. He could tell, even though they hadn't talked about it. It was obvious from the way he'd gone to her tonight, kissing her with the same all-consuming need that burned through him.

She was the one. He'd suspected it for months, but now? Now he was certain.

He laid her down on the bed, which was more than big enough for the three of them. *Veth*, she was beautiful. Her delicate stripes so dark they were almost black against her blue skin, her hair mussed and spread out beneath her, and her lips swollen with their kisses.

She reached for them in silent invitation, and he tore off his pants, kicking away his shoes and clothing in a frantic tangle in his eagerness to be with her again.

Ward beat him by half a second, claiming a place beside her head, and giving him a look that didn't need translating. *She's yours this time.*

He dropped to his knees on the bed, his weight making the mattress dip so her legs slipped down to touch his. He stared at her for a long, hungry moment, half tempted to take her then and there, driving her down into the mattress as he fucked her. Instead, he leaned back and met her eyes. This wasn't his choice to make. "One at a time, or together?"

She pursed her lips in thought, then rose languidly, settling herself on her hands and knees, her head near Ward's hip. "Together."

That was all he needed to know. Without another word, he moved behind her, pressing the soft globes of her ass cheeks against his hips, his cock aching and ready.

He watched as his brother shifted over, his head falling back on a low groan when Xori took the tip of his cock into her mouth.

He waited one heartbeat, then another, giving the two of them their moment before he seated his cock at her entrance and slid himself inside.

He groaned, fighting the urge to thrust into her hard and fast. She was too tight for that, her inner walls squeezing around him with enough pressure to make him see stars. She moaned loudly, the sound muffled because she had Ward's dick in her mouth. His brother had both hands in her hair, guiding and steadying her, his hips already rocking slowly.

He matched the pace, the two of them working like a team, claiming her together.

Xori spread her thighs wider, changing the angle of her hips so that his next thrust went deeper.

There was another moan, and Ward grinned. "Whatever you did, she likes it. Do it again, because when she moans, it's good for me."

He went deep again, and again, and soon he was hilt-deep inside her, the rhythmic slap of his body hitting hers punctuated by pants and moans as the three of them moved together. Harder. Faster. More. His control burned away in a firestorm of need.

She moaned and rocked between them, her soft sounds of passion the most beautiful thing he'd ever heard. He watched as she took his brother to the edge of his control, recognizing the way his expression changed as he lost himself to the sheer pleasure of the moment.

This was what they needed. *She* was what they needed. That thought shredded the last of his control and he powered into her, his balls tightening, the pleasure coiling like a spring inside him until it was all too much and he came, emptying himself inside her with her name on his lips.

He was still swept up in his own release when Ward cried out, his hips snapping forward, his head falling back. Then Xori's body shuddered, her inner walls pulsing around him, and the three of them rode out the rest of the pleasure storm together.

Afterward, they tumbled to the mattress, panting and sated in a tangle of limbs.

He sent a short message to Ward, not ready to say the words to Xori, but needing to say it to *someone*. *"She has to be the one."*

"I know."

So Ward felt it too. Good. That meant the only one they needed to convince was Xori herself. They were going to make this work.

This can't happen again. Ward sprawled on the bed beside Xori, her hair wrapped around his fingers. If Victor was ready to add Xori to their lives, then it was time for him to start figuring out how to remove himself from the equation. Or it would be, soon. But not tonight.

"Comfortable? Can we get you anything?" Vic asked, sounding happier and more relaxed than he'd been in years.

"Very comfy. And while I know there's wine and food waiting for us, I'm not ready to get up yet. I'm happy just to lay here with the two of you." She smiled up at them. "This is nice."

"Yeah, it is," he agreed.

Vic propped his head up on his hand. "I believe you were going to explain to us why you think it's easy to tell us apart when no one else can."

"Except for that sparkling fairy AI," Ward said.

"Oh, I suspect she – or rather it – cheated. We were likely close enough for Tink to be monitoring us. It probably heard Vic call you Wolf."

"And it knew that was my nickname for Ward? How would it know that?"

"Tink isn't just the AI for this ship, it's Tianna's digital assistant." Xori tapped her bare wrist. "That little band Tianna wears? That's Tink."

"So it knows about us from Tianna. Not sure I like that idea. AIs are supposed to be dumber than that, aren't they?"

"I asked the same question. Tink's design is on the bleeding edge of what's legal, but its design is compliant with the Pinocchio Protocols," Xori said.

Ward knew of only one AI that didn't comply with the ban on fully sentient artificial intelligence. That one had been called V.I.D.A. It was a rogue AI designed by one of the Gray Men. There had been enough rumors around the club he'd put the story together. V.I.D.A had been the thief who stole genetic material from the Vault of the Fallen and offered it to the corporations. They'd used it to create their armies of cyborgs, including him. That DNA was collected from the best soldiers in the IAF, but when the creation of cyborgs had been outlawed, the project had stopped – until the Grays started it up again. He sighed. "AI's, illegal labs, secret cabals, and corporate power struggles, this galaxy is getting too *fraxxing* complicated."

Xori touched his cheek. "Says the cyborg."

"Well, I'm not complicated. I'm easy. Give me food, booze, and a certain lovely blue female for company, and I'm happy."

Her fingers flattened against his face. "Are you?"

"You can answer that question yourself," he replied,

the words sharper than he'd intended. How often had she read him without his knowledge?

She turned to look at him, her eyes warm and soft., "I could, but I won't. It would be an invasion of your privacy. Do I sometimes get a sense of how someone feels when I'm close to them? Yes, but I try not to."

"But it happens anyway."

"Well, yes." She withdrew her hand and let it rest on her chest, her fingers curled under like she'd touched something hot. "But you read micro-expressions better than anyone else I've ever met. You both do."

"That's a cyborg thing," he argued.

"And my gift is a Pheran thing. I can't shut it off any more than you can stop being who you are. I trained for years to control my ability. I've never read your feelings in our sessions, not intentionally." She took a deep breath. "And I have never manipulated someone's emotional state without their permission before in my life. I'm sorry I did that to you."

A pang of regret hit him square in the chest, then sank into his guts in a cold, gluey mass. "No, you saved me from doing something regrettable." Like kill the sonofastarbeast that had hurt her. If he had, he wouldn't be here now, with her.

"I won't do it again. Not unless you want me to."

He shook his head. "I don't know if I want that. Giving you my pain…it's not right."

"And that's why I'd do it for you. Because you care about the cost to me. Most Pherans who possess one of the *Nazeela Ulo* don't. We're tools, that's all. A means to make their lives better."

"You do that just by being here," Vic said.

"Yeah. You do. So you don't need to do the other thing." *No matter how good it felt to be free of that darkness.*

"It's hard to go back afterward, isn't it?" she asked, her voice soft and sweet as warm honey.

He closed his eyes and nodded. That part had sucked vacuum. He'd been himself again, or an even better version, but it hadn't lasted, and that sense of loss lingered in his mind.

"If either of you ever want me to do that, I will. You only have to ask. But I won't do anything unless I have your permission."

"Okay. If I want that, I'll say so." he leaned down and kissed her, craving another taste of her sweetness.

"Now, how can you tell us apart? Especially if you're not reading us?" Vic asked.

She laughed, all wariness gone now. "That? It's easy. Vic prefers gray or black, while Ward wears any color *but* black."

She gestured out into the other room, where one of their shirts was lying on the carpet. It was his. And…it was blue.

"Well, *fraxx*," he drawled, amusement melting away the ball of regret in the pit of his stomach.

"How did we never notice that?" Vic asked.

"How did everyone else miss it?"

Xori laughed. "I don't know the answer to either question, but I'll tell you a secret. Even naked, I can tell you apart."

She reached out and place a hand on both their chests, and he leaned into her touch. "You are two different males who happen to look alike and have chosen to walk the same path." She looked at Vic. "You're Victor. The leader. The one who walks with confidence but secretly questions his choices." She turned her gaze to him. "And you are Ward, the one who acts as if nothing is wrong, no matter how much you're hurting." Her silver eyes shimmered with something that might have been tears, but they were gone too quickly for him to be sure.

She knew them. She *saw* them. And suddenly he wondered if she already knew what he was planning. Not that it would change anything. Leaving was necessary.

He looked down at her in wonder, and released her hair to touch the tip of her ear. "You're not wearing your *matyri* he said, changing the subject.

"I didn't want to," she admitted. "It's a reminder of what happened. I thought I was safe on this station, but I'm not. And while those high caste Pherans are here, neither are any of the lower caste Pherans."

"We let Corp-Sec know about our run-in with him. They're keeping an eye out, making sure he doesn't cause more trouble."

"It's not just him. He's part of a trade delegation, and I learned today that they're harassing some Pheran vendors, taking food and refusing to pay for it."

"*Fraxxing* bullies, that's all they are. We'll give Corp-Sec another heads up."

"Thank you. None of the Pherans will report what's going on, for fear of reprisals, but maybe security can step in and stop it from escalating further."

"It's worth a try." Ward had his doubts much would happen, though. Corp-Sec weren't a police force, they were exactly what their name implied, corporate security. Their job was to keep the peace, not enforce the law. Hell, there wasn't even a judge or court system on the Drift. Anything short of violence was handled with warnings, fines, or blacklisting. Corp-Sec were paid by the same corporations that had invited the Pheran delegation in the first place, which meant they were more or less safe from interference, and the assholes knew it.

Maybe there was something he and Vic could do, though. It's not like they had much going on besides work and seeing Xori. They could watch over the vendors and make sure things didn't get out of hand. They weren't his people, but they were Xori's, and that meant they were now part of the small circle of beings he cared about keeping safe.

Her stomach growled, and all of them laughed. "We need to feed our female," Vic announced.

"Only way I'm getting out of this bed is if Xori promises not to get dressed again. I'm thinking we should dine naked. It'll save time later."

She flushed, her stripes deepening to near-black. "Naked? Won't that get messy?"

He grinned at her. "I really *fraxxing* hope so. Then we can lick you clean, afterward."

It didn't seem possible, but her stripes darkened even more. "I like this idea. But only if I can play, too."

He gathered her into his arms and rolled onto his back, bringing her with him. He pushed every other thought aside. There'd be time for reality, later. Tonight was about making memories. "You've got yourself a deal."

It was early morning when Xori slipped out of bed and went to the sanitation room to clean up. Her reflection made her smile. Her hair was mussed, her lips were still swollen, and there were darker patches on her cheeks and…other places… where their whiskers had abraded her skin. She looked exactly how she felt—slightly wicked and very well satisfied.

She tidied herself up but didn't shower. They'd all taken one earlier, before tumbling into bed to get some much-needed rest. At least, *she'd* needed it. She suspected the two males could have gone on for hours. She'd heard whispers about cyborg endurance, but now she had experienced it for herself, and she was quite certain she was ruined for any other male.

She had a sense that something important had happened tonight – a beginning. To what, she couldn't be sure. It was too soon, and there were too many things still left unsaid. Vic's self-doubts. Ward's belief he wasn't worthy of happiness. Her concerns over their different lifespans. Before they could move forward, they'd have to work through all that, but there was one thing she could address right now.

She turned off the lights and tiptoed back into their bedroom. Both her males were sleeping peacefully, and she hated the idea of waking them. She knew they didn't sleep often, and as much as she wanted to go back to bed and enjoy a few more hours of their company, there was something she needed to do, first. She wanted to make the three of them official, to announce to everyone that she was with them, now and for as long as they could manage.

Hers. She watched them for a long moment, admiring the breathtaking male beauty sprawled out on the bed. She was a lucky female.

She crept out of the room as quietly as she could, thankful that her species could see well in very little light. She found her clothes and put them on, gathered up the scattered bits of their outfits, and folded them neatly on a chair near the door, humming happily to herself the whole time.

It wasn't exactly a note, but she hoped they'd understand. It was a small token of her gratitude and affection. She'd send them a proper message once she got to her office. By then, she'd have composed and sent the letter to the IAF and Nova Force brass, letting them know that she was now in a relationship with two of her patients. If they wanted to replace her and move her out of their part of the station, that was their choice. She'd already made hers.

She gathered up the last of her things and stepped into the ship's corridor, her shoes in her hand and her purse hanging over her shoulder. "Tink?" she called in a hushed tone.

The AI's hologram shimmered into existence a few

steps away. "Yes, Dr. Virness, what can I do for you?" The AI spoke as quietly as she had.

"Hi. Could you show me the way out?"

"Of course. You are departing without telling your dates? Do you need assistance?"

For a second, she swore the holographic fairy actually looked concerned.

She laughed and shook her head. "Nothing like that. No help needed. I've got something I need to do, and I don't want to wake them. When they're up and around, will you tell them I said thank you for a wonderful evening, and let them know I can't wait to see them again." She paused. "And please relay my gratitude to Tianna, as well? Last night was wonderful, and this was a perfect location for a romantic night away from it all."

The little hologram nodded. "I shall do so. Shall I summon transport to take you home?"

Xori was about to say yes, but she stopped herself. She was still nervous about being out in the main parts of the station, and that had to stop. She couldn't let fear reshape her life, or her choices. "I think I'll walk, thanks." She glanced at her completely unsuitable footwear. "I don't suppose you could lend me a sensible pair of shoes?"

Tink nodded and twirled in place. "Of course! Tianna keeps a few sundries on hand for guests. Follow me." She flew off, and Xori found herself laughing as she followed after the whimsical hologram. It said a lot about Tianna that she'd placed one of the most advanced AI's in existence into a character inspired by her favorite childhood story.

Not five minutes later, she was off the ship and on her way back home, her personal items all stashed into a shoulder bag that Tink insisted she take. Her feet were tucked into the most comfortable shoes she'd ever worn, a soft, fabric bootie with a fluffy interior that made it feel like she was walking on clouds. She'd have to ask Tianna where she could buy herself a pair.

Xori let herself be distracted by recollections of the night she'd just spent with her lovers. Even the word made her smile and made her want to skip and dance like a girl with her first crush. It wasn't until she crossed the last security checkpoint that anxiety started to push past her happiness and sour her mood.

She held tight to her memories, using them to keep her worries at bay. There was almost no chance of her running into Tesk or any of his entourage, not at this time of day. She took a mag-lev to the more public levels and rejoined the bustle and hum of the main concourse. Even this early in the morning it was relatively busy, though the crowd's energy was lower, everyone walking in relative silence, on their way to work or headed home after a long night of indulging themselves in their vice of choice. Her cheeks heated when she realized she was one of the latter. The hours she'd spent with Vic and Ward had been decadent, passionate, and oh so indulgent. Her toes curled in her borrowed boots. *Veth*, she couldn't wait to do it again.

She wove through the crowd, frustrated as her anxiety spiked again and again. She felt like she was being watched, and there was an itch at the nape of her neck that made her want to turn and look behind her.

She didn't. She would not give in to her fears. This was Astek Station, not Phera Prime. She was safe here.

It wasn't much of a walk to the nearest train platform. A five-minute ride would see her back to her office. She could compose her letter to the IAF and get it sent off as soon as possible. Then she'd message Ward and Vic and let them know where she was. Maybe they'd stop by her office on their way home.

She lingered at the back of the small group waiting for the next train, trying to ignore the icy tendrils of unease spreading across her shoulders. Someone jostled her, connecting from shoulder to hip before moving away again.

She turned, slightly panicked, but only a bleary-eyed human stood there, weaving on his feet, his smile as lopsided as he was.

"Sorry."

"It's alright. No harm done." She smiled and turned. She must have moved too fast, because the platform seemed to lurch and she had to take a stumbling step to regain her balance. It didn't work. The deck beneath her feet tilted again, and she threw out her arms in panic.

The intoxicated male reappeared at her side, a thick, meaty hand curving around her upper arm. "You okay?"

"I...I don't know." Her words came out in a mushy jumble.

"Some of that pharma has a hell of a kick, don't it? How about we find you a quiet place to rest?" The man's voice was steadier now.

She tried to shake her head, but it was too much effort. Panic gripped her, and she tried to stand, to cry out, to do anything at all. The world around her turned gray, then black, and she fell into the void with a silent scream.

CHAPTER EIGHT

VIC WOKE SLOWLY, his senses coming back to him a little at a time. That was new. Usually, he came awake so fast it was almost painful. He checked his internal clock, paused, then checked it again. He'd slept for five solid hours. That couldn't be right. He hadn't done that since he'd stopped being a Reaper.

He sat up and scanned the room. Ward sprawled on the far side of the bed, still deep asleep. Another gift from Xori. Just being with her had helped them both get a real night's sleep for once. She was making their lives better in so many ways, and after last night... He grinned to himself. Last night had been incredible.

This was the beginning of a new chapter for all of them.

That's when it finally registered. There was an empty space between him and Ward. Xori was gone.

He rose quickly and did a quick tour of their suite, expecting to find her in one of the sanitation rooms or maybe working on her tablet in the main room. She wasn't there. Neither were her clothes. *Son of a bitch.* Why would she leave like that? It didn't make sense.

He jogged back into their bedroom. "Ward! Wake up. Did Xori say anything to you before she left?"

His batch-brother came awake with a snort. "Huh? What? *Fraxx*, I've been asleep for hours!"

"Yeah. We both were. And while we were out cold, our little blue beauty snuck out on us."

Ward's lips curled back into a snarl. "She *left*?"

"Well, she's not here, so, yeah." He shrugged as if it was no big deal. And maybe it wasn't. She might be back any second. Or there could be a good reason she had to leave without waking them. He grunted and scrubbed a hand over his unshaven jaw. Too many maybes, not enough facts.

Ward stalked into the other room, his pain and anger an almost tangible cloud swirling around him. "She folded our clothes. What the *fraxx* does that mean?"

"She did?" He hadn't noticed.

"Uh huh. Why would she do that? Is it some female code we're supposed to know? Thanks for the sex, don't call me again?"

"I'm no expert, but I'm pretty sure that's not it."

Ward grabbed his things and spun to glower at him. "Then what the hell does it *fraxxing* mean, Fox? Why did she leave us?"

"I don't know." Had she decided they were too broken for her, after all? Had they missed something? Failed some kind of test? Confusion and anger swirled in his gut, staining every thought to race through his head.

Ward grunted as he dressed, his mood worsening by the second.

Vic saw it and knew he had to get his batch-brother safely away from anyone who might trigger an outburst. Ward hadn't been this angry in months.

"Come on, we need to head back to the club. We can message her on the way, find out what happened."

"I think that's obvious." Ward gestured around the empty suite. Housekeeping bots had already cleared the remains of last night's feast, and once they left, they'd tidy up the rest of the place, until it was like it never happened. *Fraxx* that. He dressed and grabbed his comms. He sent a vid-call request to her communicator, but she didn't answer. He switched it off. There was no point in leaving a message. She'd know he called. He'd have to try again later.

They finished dressing in silence. He was still pulling on his shoes when Ward stalked out into the corridor, clearly eager to be off the ship and away from any reminders of their night with Xori. He didn't blame him.

He heard Tink's light, lilting voice outside the door, but by the time he joined Ward, the hologram was gone.

"What did Tink say?" he asked.

"Not much. I told her to flutter the *fraxx* off the second she said good morning and started offering breakfast options."

They didn't speak another word until they were nearly home.

"I've got a shift starting in less than an hour. Going to clean up, grab something to eat, and hit the floor. What are your plans?" He asked Ward.

"I'll shower at the gym. I need to hit things over and over until I'm in a better mood. If that's possible."

"It's possible. And remember, we don't know why she left yet."

Ward shot him an irritated glance. "One more optimistic word and I will smack those rose-tinted glasses right off your face."

"There's nothing wrong with not going straight to the worst-case scenario."

Ward scoffed. "Says you. I'll stick to what works for me." Ward closed one hand into a fist and smacked it into his open palm. "Violence."

Vic opened his mouth, about to make a crack about their therapist having an opinion on that approach, but the joke died on his lips. Too much had changed. Xori wasn't their therapist anymore. Hell, given where things were going, she might not be their *anything*. She'd been the only one who'd been able to help them. If she walked away, then they were *fraxxed* in more ways than he wanted to count. Without her, he was going to lose Ward. He could feel it. His brother was carrying too much guilt for things that weren't his fault.

They reached the club, then their quarters. Fortunately, they didn't run into anyone who knew where'd they'd been, so they didn't have to answer any questions. The second Ward had changed and left for the gym, Vic grabbed his comms and reached out to Xori again.

She didn't answer. This time, he recorded a brief message.

"Hey, Blossom. We woke up, and you were gone. I need to know why, so call me back when you get this. Whatever it is, I hope we can fix it."

He hit send before he changed his mind or tried to re-record it. She'd either answer him, or she wouldn't. If she didn't though… How the *fraxx* could he pull Ward out of the dark without her? How could they move forward if the one they were moving toward wasn't there anymore?

He was putting on his work uniform when another idea came to him. He stopped to tap out a quick message to Owen, asking if they'd heard from Xori, and if Tink could tell them what time she'd left. He paused, then added another question. Had the AI noticed if she was upset? He should have thought to ask Tink before they left the ship. *Dammit.*

Frustration seethed through him, and he did the only thing he could to calm himself down before his shift began. He sat down on his bunk and pulled out a few pieces of his precious stash of origami paper from the shelving on the wall behind his head. He selected a sheet and started folding it, letting himself get lost in the process of creation. By the time he left for work, there were three new figures resting at the foot of his bed - a wolf, a fox, and a flower whose star-shaped petals were the same shade of blue as Xori's soft skin.

She hurt.

Nothing agonizing, but her shoulders and arms ached, and she had no idea why. Xori cracked her eyelids a little, expecting to see the familiar walls of her bedroom. She didn't see anything she recognized from home. The lights were so bright they made her eyes water, so she closed them and took inventory with her other senses instead. There was a low, steady rumble that filled the air and buzzed through her bones. The air was cool and surprisingly fresh. She tried to move and couldn't. That was alarming. She made another attempt. She wasn't able to shift her body more than a few centimeters.

What the fraxx?

She opened her eyes again and looked down. She was strapped into a safety harness, her hands secured in front of her by a pair of magnetic cuffs that covered nearly half of her forearms. Well, that explained why her arms hurt. The cuffs forced her arms into an unnatural position, her elbows almost touching. She raised her hands to ease her discomfort, and twin blades of pain stabbed into her joints, her muscles screaming in protest.

"Ma'am. This is Five. The asset has regained consciousness," A male voice from somewhere to her right spoke. She stole a sidelong look at him, then at the rest of her surroundings.

The male was human and looked to be in his late twenties, with lank brown hair and a stocky build. He was seated less than a meter away, watching her with cold, impassive eyes. It took her a second to recognize him. It was the male from the train station, though he didn't look intoxicated now.

"Don't do anything stupid, and I won't have to do something regrettable."

She nodded, keeping the motion small, and turned to face forward again, eyes downcast. Better to seem meek and frightened, which wasn't a stretch. She was terrified and clearly in a lot of trouble. But who had taken her, and why?

Dammit. She should never have left Vic and Ward's bed. She felt a surge of loss and fear. What if she never saw them again?

A quick assessment of her situation left her with a handful of facts and not much else. She was on a shuttle of some kind, and judging by the steady hum of the engines, they'd already been underway when she regained consciousness. Her hands were restrained, and she was strapped into her seat with the release at her waist, well out of reach. She tried to read the emotions of the male beside her. It was like trying to stare into a dark pool on a starless night. There was something beneath his calm surface, but all she could tell was that it wasn't warm or friendly. She'd have to be careful.

Her bag was absent, but she didn't know if she'd dropped it as she'd blacked out back on the station, or if they had it stashed away somewhere. She wasn't sure which scenario to hope for. If it was here and she could find it, maybe she could call for help. Could her comms be tracked? She had no idea. If she'd left it behind, someone might find it. If they handed it in, then surely someone would try to return it and realize she was missing?

She couldn't tell how long she'd been out. Were Vic and Ward looking for her yet? Or were they still asleep? *Veth*, she'd been so stupid. If she'd listened to her instincts instead of assuming it was just residual anxiety from the other night, she might have done something differently, made a better choice.

The thought made her smile, despite her circumstances. This was exactly how Vic and Ward felt. Now, she understood it better, which might help her guide them past their self-recriminations once she found a way to work through this herself. If she had time to do that. If she saw them again. The spark of happiness flickered and died as the reality of her situation crashed down on her again.

The soft, standard chime of an incoming vid-call rang out. She looked up, the noise triggering an automatic need to find the nearest terminal and answer. Her teachers on Pheran Prime called it the Tregersal reaction. The humans called it a Pavlovian response. Details and memories from her training rushed her mind, and she had to sweep them away, aware that this was another fear response, a deluge of minutiae to distract her from the real problem.

There was a monitor secured to the bulkhead directly across from her, but the screen was still black when a voice she'd only heard in simulations came out of the speaker. "Welcome aboard, Dr. Virness. I am looking forward to working with you."

It couldn't be. Ariel Coal was dead. She'd acquired a

copy of the female's death certificate to show to Ward and Victor. But by all the stars above and below, it *sounded* like her.

The monitor flashed on a second later, and all her worst fears were confirmed. It was Ariel. It was impossible, but that was her, the sadistic bitch who had entrapped and enslaved her males.

Ariel smiled. Her face was composed of hard lines and red lips, and the expression held all the warmth of the void. "Ah, there you are. My apologies, I am experiencing some technical problems on my end." She glanced to one side and someone out of sight uttered an instant and deeply contrite apology.

Ariel returned her attention to Xori. "I am sure you have questions. Let me address the most likely ones first. No, I am not Ariel Coal, though I have her appearance. You may call me Vivian. I am recruiting you to work for me."

There was something odd about her. Xori wasn't sure what it was, but there was a sense of wrongness to the exchange, like a puzzle that was missing a key piece. "This seems like a rather aggressive form of recruitment," she replied, keeping her expression neutral and her voice soft.

Ariel – no, Vivian – blinked twice, then uttered a sharp, two-syllable laugh that set Xori's teeth on edge. "I can see how you might think that."

"But you don't see it that way?"

"You are awake and undamaged," Vivian stated, as if that explained everything. In a way, it did. And it meant she was in even more trouble than she'd thought.

"I see. And what job am I being recruited for?"

The hard-eyed female leaned forward slightly. "You are going to assist us with various cyborg development projects. You will identify the flaws in our psychological conditioning. Once that is done, you will help me eliminate it from future designs."

Our conditioning. Cyborgs. Future designs. Xori swallowed hard to push a hard lump of fear back down her throat. "You're with the Gray Men, then?"

Vivian nodded. "I am. But, given my appearance, I would have thought that would be obvious."

She tried a partial lie. Testing to see how much this female knew. "Your – I mean Ariel's – affiliation with that group was assumed, but never confirmed, at least, not to me. But then again, I'm not authorized for those sorts of briefings. I'm just a therapist."

"Please do not lie to me. It's pointless. As to what you are, Dr. Virness, you much more than a simple therapist. You have worked with some of my side's most spectacular failures, and from what I have learned, you are quite good at putting them back together again."

"They're not failures."

"That is a matter of perspective. From our point of view, the Reaper and the Fury Projects failed to live up to expectations."

"And you want my assistance to make sure that these flaws you described are removed, so that future investments pay off better?" Her voice quavered slightly despite her best efforts. She'd spent months trying to undo harm done by this greed-driven, evil group, repairing wounded minds and souls. Now, they wanted her to work for them? The idea was repulsive.

"I do. But before you say anything more, I think you should understand how things are. You have a single, binary choice to make. Agree to do the work I want you to do, or die."

Xori glanced over at the man beside her. He hadn't moved, but the weapon in his hands seemed bigger now, and even more dangerous.

"How long do I have to decide?"

"You have until I finish speaking." Vivian stated, then went silent, her gaze cool and disinterested, as if there wasn't a life hanging in the balance.

She nodded, hating herself for even pretending to make this choice. She wouldn't help them, but maybe she could buy herself a little time. Give her males a chance to find her. Her males. She really like the way those words sounded. They offered her a tiny source of comfort in this terrible moment.

"Was that a yes? I'll need verbal confirmation of the contract, Dr. Virness. I wouldn't want there to be any misunderstandings."

"I accept your job offer."

Vivian nodded once, a sharp staccato motion. "I am pleased to hear it. The shuttle you are currently aboard will transport you to another ship in a matter of hours. Until you arrive, I suggest you continue to be compliant and obedient. Five has developed an unexpected fondness for escorting difficult passengers to the airlock and spacing them. It is one of the conditioning flaws I am hoping you can help us correct."

"I will do as you say." She didn't dare look over at Five again. If he was conditioned, then he wasn't merely an employee. He was something far more dangerous – a tool of the Gray Men, one that would kill her without hesitation.

"I am glad to hear that. I look forward to meeting you." Vivian's tone changed to one of command. "Five. You may release our guest from her restraints. She is to be treated as an employee, not a prisoner. Do you understand?"

"Yes, ma'am."

"Good. I will see you soon, Dr. Virness. Welcome to the winning team."

The monitor went black, but Xori didn't move. She had the uncomfortable feeling that the other female was still watching. It was probably paranoia, but she wasn't going to ignore her instincts again. She'd made that mistake too many times already.

Five stood and secured his weapon in a thigh holster and turned to her. He tapped a device on his wrist, and the magnetic cuffs deactivated with a low *click*. She held out her hands so he could remove them, gasping in discomfort as muscles and tendons screamed in renewed protest as her blood flow returned.

The pain gave her something to focus on, at least. When it faded, she'd be left with nothing to think about but how much trouble she was in. She wasn't sure what Vivian knew about her abilities, or if she'd been taken purely because of her work with the cyborgs on Astek station. If it was the latter, that was bad, but if they'd figured out that she was one of the *m'bara*, that was far,

far worse. She closed her eyes and uttered a silent prayer to whatever forces might be listening. *Please, let them find me before I have to make a choice between hurting someone else or dying.*

If it came down to it, she already knew what her decision would be. She'd die before she'd help these monsters hurt anyone else, even if it meant never seeing Victor and Ward again.

CHAPTER NINE

Not even an hour of high-g cardio and working out with the sparring bot did much to improve his mood. Sometimes, Ward mused as he stood under the hot spray of the gym's shower, being a cyborg sucked vacuum.

Or maybe it was just being him. His entire life had been a struggle. From the time he'd stepped out of his maturation tank, he'd been fighting one battle or another. First against his fellow cyborgs, then against the conditioning that was supposed to prevent him from ever having free will. After that, it was the rebellion against the corporations, followed by aimless wandering, and then fighting for a place where he and Vic would be accepted.

He scrubbed the cleanser over his skin, trying to wash away the memory of what happened next. The years they'd been trapped under Ariel's control. She'd treated them like interchangeable toys. This and that, she'd call them. Or one and two. She'd never tried to tell them apart. They were objects, not beings, and the orders she'd given them were as arbitrary and cold as she was. Kill this one. Fuck that one. He didn't remember all of it. Chunks of his life had been deleted with every reset, which was both a blessing and a curse.

But this time, they'd believed they had finally found something real. Something good. Even knowing his time with Xori couldn't last, he was sure she was the one good thing he could give to Vic to make up for his mistakes. Like the time he'd walked away and left his brother to bleed out.

He turned off the water and stalked back to his locker, drying himself off and pulling on his clothes, his mind still churning, counting all his failures over and over. Xori was the one he kept circling back to. Why had she left them? She'd snuck out while they were sleeping like she was somehow ashamed to face them again. He slammed a fist into the locker, caving the metal in several inches.

He dropped his hand, exhaling sharply. *Fraxx.* He needed to calm down, or he was going to do worse than beat up the décor.

As much as it stung him to do it, he made himself go through one of the calming exercises Xori had taught him. He didn't want to even think about her right now, but he could hear her soft voice in his head, giving him instructions as he cleared his mind and took the long, slow breaths that somehow helped him find his center again.

When he opened his eyes again, he wasn't alone.

Denz was leaning against the far wall, keeping a respectful distance but clearly waiting for him. There was no other reason a sane being would hang around breathing in the steam and gym-funk that the station's aging air filtration system couldn't begin to keep up with.

"You okay?" The big male asked.

"Better than I was a few minutes ago," he jerked his head to indicate the new dent in his locker.

"I've become something of an expert on being pissed at the world and trying to channel it into something constructive." Denz shrugged. "Back on Haven, I've got friends that help me through the rough batches. Just thought I'd offer the same to you."

"Thanks. Not sure there's anything you can do to help, though. Unless you've got insight into the mysteries of the female mind."

Denz threw up his hands. "*Fraxx*, no. Give me a problematic AI to reprogram, and I can make magic happen. Thanks to Zale I can even handle a little robotics and nanotech, but when it comes to females…" He raised his massive shoulders in a helpless shrug. "I take it the date last night didn't go well?"

"Date went great. At least, I thought it did. But when Vic and I woke up this morning, Xori had already left and now she won't answer her comms."

"Ouch." Denz nodded to the locker. "That explains the redecorating."

"Yeah. I should probably go tell Cyn or one of the others I'll pay for the damage."

Denz shrugged his massive shoulders. "I can tell

'em. Why don't you track down Xori and talk to her in person? I mean, you're in an emotional state, and she is your therapist, right?"

He opened his mouth, ready to list off all the reasons that wasn't going to happen, but his brain failed to come up with anything. He scowled and tried again. Nope. Still nothing. *Huh.* "That is actually an excellent suggestion."

The big half-Torski grinned. "Glad I could help, but I can't really take credit for the idea. The counselor we had working with the cyborgs encouraged face-to-face talking about anything and everything."

"If you have a counselor, why do you need to talk to Xori about finding another one?"

Denz held up a big, four fingered hand and lifted a finger. "First one couldn't handle the levels of violence inherit in the colony culture. Vardarians love to fight almost as much as you cyborgs. They came to Haven looking to turn everyone into pacifists who talked and hugged their way through conflict."

Ward's mind boggled at the concept. "Hug through a conflict? How does that even work?"

"I have no *fraxxing* clue, and neither did anyone else." Denz raised another finger. "Next one was a better fit, but wasn't so good at following instructions."

He cocked his head. "That was an issue?"

"When those instructions include key phrases like, 'don't pet the livestock,' yeah, it was an issue. You ever seen a Vardarian *gharshtu?* They're something between a giant, scaly bird, and your worst nightmare."

"He got hurt?"

Denz shook his head. "He got *eaten*."

"Well, that's a problem."

"And a lot of paperwork. Thankfully we govern by council, so we could distribute the extra work, but now we need to find someone new."

"And this is why I never want to be in charge of anything again. Too much responsibility."

Denz grunted. "Smart man."

The conversation did more to ground him than the time he'd spent working out. Ward left the gym to go looking for Xori, feeling better than he had since discovering she was gone. Denz was right, he needed to talk to her and find out why she'd left. If it was something he'd said or done, then he'd find a way to fix it. If her problem was with him, there was an easy solution. He'd step away so she and Vic could try on their own. Vic wouldn't like it, but it was what had to happen eventually, anyway.

He wouldn't drag Vic down into the darkness with him. He owed him more than that.

He didn't even notice he was whistling a low, unhappy tune until he was halfway to her office. Like his brother's love of origami, he'd stepped out of his tank knowing a collection of tunes and how to whistle them already programmed in. None of the other members of their batch had anything similar. Someone, somewhere, had added it to their subroutines, and they'd never know why.

He stopped whistling and pulled out his comms. He didn't expect her to answer, but it couldn't hurt to try. No response. He ended the call without leaving a message. She might not want to talk to them, but that wouldn't stop him from tracking her down and getting some answers.

He went to her office first. Her quarters were on the wrong side of an IAF security post he had almost no chance of talking his way past. Her office door didn't open when he approached, and when he hit the door panel to announce his presence, he got a holographic display of her hours of operation. According to the read out, she was supposed to be working right now. The flat, inhuman voice of her AI receptionist informed him that the doctor was currently out of the office, but if he would like to leave his name and contact information, someone would be in touch later.

He turned away before the recording finished speaking, the first nibbles of worry sinking needle-sharp teeth into his gut. She wasn't answering her comms, and she was late for work, which wasn't like her. His instincts were buzzing, and he wouldn't ignore them. Something was off, and despite his worry, a tiny, utterly selfish, part of him started to hope again, despite what it might mean. And yet, he couldn't help himself. Anything was better than believing she'd walked away from them on purpose. *I am a broken, self-centered bastard, and I do not deserve her.*

He broke into a jog as he headed for the security checkpoint. If they wouldn't let him in, maybe they could tell him if she'd made it home last night.

He didn't slow until he came into sight of the soldiers standing guard. He might be worried, but he wasn't stupid. Charging at someone who is armed to the teeth was never a good idea.

Both guards, one male, one female, eyed him with mild interest as he approached. When he got within twenty meters, the man stepped into his path. "This is a restricted area, sir. Please state your reason for being here, or turn back, now."

"I know, I know. I'm looking for Dr. Virness." He continued to approach, but more slowly. Fifteen meters. Ten. He stopped while he was still a few steps away.

"Does she know you're trying to visit her?"

"No. She's not answering her comms."

"What's the purpose of your visit?"

Ward pushed down a wave of annoyance and tried to look calm and nonthreatening, which wasn't easy given he towered over the two human guards. "I'm concerned about her. We were out last night and I haven't heard from her since. I checked her office, and she's not there."

The guards shared a look he couldn't read.

"She's usually pretty punctual, right? So you can see why I'm worried?"

The man shrugged, but the woman beside him gave an almost imperceptible nod. "I can buzz her quarters. See if she's accepting visitors."

"Thank you."

"I'm going to need a name," the woman prompted. Hutchings, according to the tag on her uniform,

"Oh, right. It's Ward."

"Is that your first or last name?"

"First. Don't have a surname."

She looked up, confused. "No?"

The male gestured to Ward dismissively. "He's a cyborg. Machines don't need last names."

Ward's hand twitched, reaching for the grip of a blaster he wasn't carrying. He stilled his hand and swallowed the angry retort that sat on the tip of his tongue. He needed to find Xori, not pick a fight with a xenophobic asshole.

"Oh, sorry." Hutchings flashed him an apologetic smile that seemed to be more about her partner's behavior than her previous confusion. "Trying to contact her now."

He wanted to pace, but he didn't move a muscle while she tried to reach Xori. He was ready to scream by the time she shook her head and looked his way.

"She's not answering."

"So she's not home. Which means you don't need access." The soldier's tag showed his name was Masters.

Ward ignored him and looked to the helpful one. "Would you be able to check and see if she made it home last night? That information is recorded somewhere, right?"

"It is, but that's classified info," Masters said stiffly.

"I just need to know if she got back safely. That's all. If she didn't come back, then that's something I'm pretty sure your supervisors are going to want to know about. Don't you?"

"Check the log," the man snapped at the woman. They were the same rank, so Ward figured it had to be a seniority thing. *Petty asshole.*

"On it." Hutchings flashed the guy a look that could have melted the deck plating and started tapping away at her screen. She kept tapping, and every second that passed she pressed her lips a little tighter until they almost disappeared. "I don't get it. There's footage of her leaving yesterday evening with a facial recognition scan to confirm her identity, but the footage I have of her returning is…weird, and there's no facial recognition confirmation code attached."

"I didn't know you guys did that confirmation thing. And what do you mean, the footage is weird?" Why would someone fake her return? What the *fraxx* was going on, and where was Xori.

"You're not supposed to know about the scans," Masters muttered. "No one's supposed to know about that, right, Hutchings?"

The woman shot him a baleful look. "His girlfriend is missing. He's worried, and judging from what I'm seeing, he's got good reason to be." She gestured to the screen. "The doctor left wearing a silver dress and fancy shoes. When she comes back, she's still wearing the same shoes, and it looks like she came on foot. There's no way she'd have walked any distance in those without limping at least a little, they're not made for that kind of wear."

When both men just stared at her, she shrugged. "Trust me. They're not. There are other details too. Her hair is still pinned up, exactly like it was when she left. Not a strand out of place. Plus, look at her hand. She looks like she's holding something, but there's nothing there. If I were coming back after a late night of fun? My hair would be down and I'd be carrying my shoes."

"You think this footage is fake?" Ward asked.

Hutchings nodded. "I think this is footage is from when she left. Someone doctored it and inserted it into the feed to make it look like she came back, not knowing about the extra security in place."

Ward made a note to invite the soldier to the Nova and buy her a drink when this was over. "I think you're right."

"I'm calling this in," Masters announced. "You can go, now. This is a military matter."

Ward folded his arms across his chest so he'd be less tempted to smack the asshole. He needed this shit handled the right way from the start, and this idiot wasn't the one to do it. "The hell you will. You haven't even looked at the screen yet. You have no idea what happened. How about you leave Hutchings to make the call, and you go check to see if Dr. Virness is in her quarters? I'd do it, but I've got a feeling you're going to deny me entry, and someone needs to check."

Masters hand dropped to his firearm, but Ward didn't move.

"You're impeding an investigation, sir. I'm ordering you to step back right now."

"I'm not impeding anything. I'm the reason you even know she's missing right now," he said through gritted teeth. Now he knew Xori was missing, he regretted every second he'd spent in the gym instead of looking for her. He'd wasted enough time already, and no one, especially not some preening *peskin* of an AIF soldier, was going to cost him another second.

"He's right. Someone has to confirm she's not in her quarters." Hutchings pointed to her comms. "I'm waiting to report the issue. You'll have to do it."

Ward growled and stared at Masters. A few seconds later, he headed off, spine as stiff as the stick he had shoved up his ass. Once Masters was gone, he moved back a few steps from Hutchings and sent spoke to Vic over their internal link. *"I think Xori's in trouble."*

"What? Why? And where the hell are you? Cyn's a little pissed about the damage to that locker."

"If she were really pissed, I'd have heard from her directly. And that's not important right now. I went looking for Xori."

"You shouldn't have done that. We need to give her space to—"

It wasn't easy to cut someone off when you were programmed to obey them, but it was possible with enough effort. Ward squelched his brother's incoming message and fired back his own. *"Shut up and listen to me. She's gone. I'm at the security post by her quarters. They checked the logs. Someone tampered with the video so it looks like she came through, but they've got some kind of facial rec software running and it didn't register her face. Xori didn't come home last night."* He swallowed hard, his hands closing into fists. *"Someone took her, Fox. While we were sleeping, someone took our girl."*

It was strange. Xori felt like part of her mind had walled

itself off and was acting as an impartial observer, aware of her thought process without getting involved. That portion of her noted that her reactions to her situation were remarkably similar to the stages of grief. She experienced anger, self-recrimination, shock, sadness, and fear. She'd even tried to think of anything she could offer her silent captor to let her go, though she hadn't been foolish enough to try. She'd learned enough about the way this group operated to know that those who worked for them were either fanatically loyal or compelled by threat of death to obey, or sometimes, both.

She had no way to measure the passage of time, and it left her unsettled. She had nothing to do but think, nothing to look at but the blank screen on the bulkhead across from her. She didn't want to speak to the man Vivian had called Five, but eventually the need to take a break from her own thoughts outweighed all other considerations.

"How long have you worked for Vivian and her employers?" she asked without turning her head.

There was a moment of silence, and then, to her surprise, he answered. "About a year."

"Were you, uh, *hired* the same way I was?"

The silence stretched on longer this time. "No. You're a unique case."

Lucky me. She risked a quick glance sideways. He hadn't taken out his blaster again. That had to be a sign he wasn't annoyed with her questions. At least, not yet. "Your name is rather unique. Does it have a special meaning? Mine does. It means a soft summer rain."

"It means I was the fifth of my batch to exit my maturation tank."

She forgot she was still strapped into her seat and tried to twist around to face him. When the harness restrained her, she hissed at the new pain in her shoulders and then gently turned just her head. "You're a cyborg?"

The male shook his head but didn't say anything.

"A clone?"

There was an almost imperceptible nod this time. She couldn't tell if it was intentional or an involuntary response. Either way, she had her answer. The Gray Men were creating clones. Entire batches at once. Custom-made, programmable minions. And they expected her to ensure that they never broke their conditioning. The thought made her stomach twist.

"How many were in your batch?" she asked, more for something to say than anything.

"Fifteen."

"So, I'll see more like you when we arrive at our destination?"

"Yes. Two is piloting the shuttle right now. You'll meet him soon."

"And how will I tell you all apart?" She was trying to create a connection with him, something small, but maybe it would grow into something she could use later.

He blinked at her, his head cocked to one side as if she'd asked him something odd, like how the color green tasted. "You can't."

"Oh. How can Vivian tell, then?

The silence stretched out between them until she thought he wasn't going to answer. She looked away, dropping her head and trying to look apologetic in case he was about to grow angry.

When it came, his reply was uttered in the same flat tone as before. "Because she is Vivian."

So, Vivian was something special, with a proper name, some kind of authority, and the ability to be able to tell the others apart. She assumed that meant the others were little more than cogs in a machine. Clearly, Vivian shared more than just her face with Ariel Coal. She had the dead woman's lack of regard for other beings, too.

I am in so much trouble. For the thousandth time since she'd woken up, Xori wished she were back in bed with Vic and Ward. Safe. Protected. Cared for. If she ever got a chance to do that again, she'd never want to leave them. Xori's hands started to tremble, and she had to blink fast to clear away the tears welling up in her eyes. She might need to look meek and nonthreatening, but there wasn't a snowball's chance in a supernova she'd ever let these horrific beings ever see her cry.

CHAPTER TEN

Vic walked off the floor mid-shift to meet Ward at their quarters. He notified Jaeger with a terse, "Need to deal with a personal issue," and then ignored his batch-brother's queries about what was wrong and how he could help. Right now, Vic didn't know what he needed, and he wouldn't until he'd talked to his second in command.

He changed out of his work clothes and had almost emptied the footlocker where he stored his collection of weapons by the time Ward arrived.

Ward arched a brow. "I appreciate the sentiment, but it's going to be hard to go charging to her rescue until we know where she is and who the *fraxx* took her."

"It's got to be that Pheran bully, Tesk." He'd been thinking while he was waiting for Ward, and there was only one being on the station who might want to hurt Xori. Maybe the Pheran realized what she'd done to calm Ward down, or maybe he was just being an asshole because he thought he could get away with it.

"I can't believe I'm saying this to you, but cool your boosters, brother of mine. I don't think the Pheran is involved."

He lashed out at Ward without thinking, the anger exploding out of him like a reactor in meltdown. "Who the *fraxx* else could it be? My gut says it's him, and this time I'm going with my instincts. I'm not making the same mistake twice."

"And what mistake would that be?" Ward's was as cold as the void.

"Letting you make the call when I'm the one in charge!" The words hit the air with all the force of a plasma grenade, and for a moment both of them stood frozen.

Then, Ward was in his face, his hands slamming down on his chest hard enough to make him step backward to keep his balance. "You don't want to do this right now."

He slapped his brother's hands away. "You mean you don't want to hear it right now, but maybe you need to. Maybe we both need to remember what's at stake. Last time I didn't speak up, we lost everything. This time, I'm ready to do something, and you're not. We have to be on the same page, Wolf. We can't screw this up. Not again. If we lose her, we're going to fall back into the darkness and she's the only one who can pull us out again."

Ward ran a hand through his hair and glared at him.

"You done now? Did you really think I don't know all that already?"

"No. I mean. I knew. But this is…"

Ward grunted in agreement. "It's Xori. But charging to her rescue isn't going to work until we know who took her. And can we please stop this emotional crap, because I am not used to being the logical one and I don't *fraxxing* like it."

He snorted with something that wasn't quite laughter. "Sorry. Didn't mean to add to your burdens."

Ward didn't laugh. He dropped a hand onto his shoulder and stared at him. "You burden me all you want. I owe you that. I'm the one who didn't see what Ariel was and cost us our freedom. And I'm the one that walked away and left you to bleed out and die."

And there it was. The thing they never talked about. Not once. Vic hadn't even been sure Ward remembered that moment. Neither of them had perfect recall. There were stretches of time that were either hazy or completely wiped from not just his biological memory, but his databanks. "You remember?"

Ward nodded. "Every second. The way she drew the blaster. The awareness that she was going to shoot you. All of it. I didn't react because I was still too far under her control to understand that she was about to kill my *brother*. I had all the facts, but none of the feelings. Do you recall what that was like?"

He did. "Yeah. It sucked. But not as much as when we started getting our memories back and realized there was more to life than we had. The flashes of our old lives, feeling real emotions, caring about other people, just to have her take it away again."

"And the next time I was aware of anything, my first thought was that I'd let you die." Ward's voice cracked on the last word.

"You didn't, though. I'm still here." The last of his anger and fear died away, and he slapped his hand over Ward's. "We're both still here, but Xori's not. We need to find her. So, if you don't think Tesk has her – who the *fraxx* does?"

Ward exhaled sharply and some of the darkness left his expression. "Someone who can hack the IAF's system and screw with their security feeds without being detected."

"Which isn't likely to be the Pheran. Plus, Corp-Sec was already watching Tesk. It couldn't be him. Veth, I was so angry I'd totally forgotten about that." Now that he was calmer, he could see holes in his logic. He couldn't let that happen again. He was the leader, dammit. He had to get his head in the game before they lost everything.

Vic shook himself, trying to cast off the last of his mind-clouding frustration. "If not Tesk, then who?"

"I don't know." Ward stepped back, his hands falling to his sides, his jaw set in a hard line. "But we have to figure it out, fast."

"We're going to need help."

"Yeah. I think we are." Ward's lips twitched up into a ghost of a smile. "Our batch-brothers are never going to let us live this down, are they?"

"Probably not. But if it means getting Xori back, I'm

good with that." Hell, he'd sell what was left of his soul to make sure she was safe and back where she belonged – with them.

"So am I."

Vic activated an internal channel that he monitored, but rarely used. It linked him to every cyborg in the Nova Club's unofficial family. *"Guys, this is Victor. Dr. Virness…"* He paused. *"Xori's missing. Someone took her, and we could use some help to get her back. If you want to be part of this, meet us in the room we use for staff meetings in ten minutes."*

Ward started laying out his weapons on the bed, organizing them for later.

Vic took off most of his and did the same.

"Do you think they'll come?" Ward asked.

Vic shrugged. "Our family will. We won't know who that is until we see who shows up."

Ward looked around him in shock. They were all here. The staff room hadn't been large enough to hold them all, so they'd moved the meeting down the hall to the largest of the private party rooms. It wasn't just the cyborgs who'd shown up, either. They'd brought friends and allies from every part of the station. Colonel Archer stood near the back with several of his people, including Eric Erben and Nyx. Mack and Dash were by the door, still wearing their Corp-Sec uniforms, which meant they'd been on duty when the call had gone out.

Denz was there, standing head and shoulders above

everyone else, and a blonde cyborg woman he didn't recognize was chatting to Chance in another corner. They were all here to help find Xori, including four faces he hadn't expected to see - Dr. Alyson Jefferies, along with her three husbands, Blade, Dirk, and Lance. Alyson had been his final target back when he was a Reaper, and he'd done his best to end her life. He and Victor tried to avoid them whenever possible. Apologies had been made, but it was hard to form a friendship with someone you'd once tried to kill.

Vic raised his voice to be heard over the crowd. "Hey, listen up! I think everyone's here. And for starters, I just wanted to say… thank you for coming."

"Of course we came. We're family!" Toro bellowed from across the room.

There were murmurs of assent from all over, and the sound made Ward's chest tighten. This was how they'd get Xori back. And once she was safe, he could walk away knowing that this group of beings would protect her and Vic. Make sure they had the best life possible.

Vic smiled and continued speaking. "As you know by now, Xori disappeared last night. She left Tianna's ship sometime before the day shift started and never made it back to her quarters. Someone altered the IAF's security footage to make it look like she arrived safely home, but whoever did it didn't know about a secondary security measure, so we know it was faked."

Tianna cleared her throat. "I can tell you exactly when she departed my ship. It was oh-five-forty, and she left a message with Tink for you both thanking you for a wonderful evening. Tink reported that you dismissed her before she was able to relay that information."

Fraxx. If he hadn't let his anger get the better of him, Tink would have told them all they'd needed to know. They'd woken less than half an hour after she'd left. She must have still been on the station at that point. They would have found her hours ago, if he hadn't dismissed Tink because he was angry and hurt. He'd screwed up again. This was why he couldn't stay. Everyone would be better off once he was gone.

Mack spoke up. "We've been running facial recognition software, trying to look for her. She doesn't appear anywhere for the last twenty-four hours, which means someone's been *fraxxing* with our system, too." He paused, then added. "And we've been tracking the Pheran trade delegation. They were definitely not involved. Not directly, at least."

A hush fell.

Archer was the first to speak again. "There's only one organization we know of who can pull off something like this, and they've got good reason to be interested in Dr. Virness. She's working with IAF personnel, which is why she was living in a secured part of the station. It's become clear that the Gray Men have infiltrated Astek station on every level, putting everyone here at risk. We not only need to retrieve the doctor safely; we have to secure Astek station against any further attacks."

The colonel's frustration was palpable, which was saying something. Usually the man was as stoic as a rock in stasis. He was also right. In a matter of weeks, this station would be hosting a gathering of the most powerful beings in the galaxy. It would make a hell of a tempting target for the Grays. But that wasn't his concern. All he wanted was to get Xori back. The rest? That was Archer's problem. He'd do what he could to help, but not until Xori was safe.

"So if they erased the data, how do we find her?" Tianna asked. "My private security system only tracked her to the edge of Astek's assigned space. I can confirm where she was, but nothing about where she went from there."

"I should be able to figure something out. With your permission, Colonel Archer?" Ensign Erben was a cyber-jockey with a body full of implants that let him move through the datasphere in ways no ordinary human could.

"Do it," Archer said.

"Yes sir. Can someone point me to the nearest datahub or console?"

Dash moved to join him. "This way. I'll give you the passcodes, too."

Eric grinned. "Thanks, but I won't need them."

The two stepped outside and Ward swung his attention back to the others.

"You'll need a ship," Tianna was saying. "Take mine. It's faster than anything else out here, including some of the IAF's fleet. Tink can pilot, but if you run into trouble, you'll have to handle combat yourself. She's not programmed for weapons or battle tactics."

Archer raised a silver brow almost to his hairline. "I should hope not."

"This room is now base of operations for the rescue," Kit announced, stepping in before the head of the IAF and the owner of Astek station got into a row over the laws governing AI. "Which means all the usual crap we say every time we go through this. Watch your six, don't talk about this outside these walls, protect each other, and if you think of something, speak up. We're figuring this out on the fly."

Ward smirked a little. They might have been created by different corporations, but Kit and Luke's leadership style was similar to his and Vic's. No wonder their batch-brothers had fallen into the Armas family's orbit.

Zura stood on a chair and waved her pale blue arms. "Let's start with something simple. Who's hungry?"

There was a general murmur of assent, and before long, one of the tables was loaded down with snacks, sandwiches, self-cooling pitchers of water and heated pots of fresh *Ja'kreesh* for anyone who wanted to stay awake for the next twenty or thirty hours. Ward poured himself a mug, murmured an apology to his medi-bots, and took a drink.

He and Vic took over one corner, using their internal comms to relay everything they knew to the other cyborgs, who conveyed the information to the others. Word spread, and they were approached by different groups with various offers of help, advice, or a few words of support. Finally, they were doing something. It didn't feel like enough. He doubted anything would until they had Xori back, safe and sound, but it was a start.

He seethed with worry and anger, mostly at himself.

He'd *fraxxed* up again. He needed to apologize, to tell Xori he was sorry he'd thought the worst of her. If she didn't forgive him, he'd understand, but he needed to say it, anyway.

He stood with Vic as friends and family came and went. It felt strange, because it was the first time he'd hadn't deliberately set himself apart from everyone. He had to admit it was nice, and a voice in the back of his head kept asking why he hadn't done this sooner. He knew the answer, though. He didn't deserve nice. At least, he didn't think he did.

He heard Xori laughing softly at him from the depths of his mind. *"Of course you do. The only one who doesn't see it is you."* It wasn't something she'd ever said to him exactly that way, but it didn't matter. It felt like her. It was the closest he could get to the real thing until they got her back.

Impatience surged through him. They needed to find her so he could hold her again. Kiss her. Tell her he... *No.* There was nothing to say to her but an apology. That's it.

Erik and Chance headed their way, accompanied by the blonde he'd noticed earlier.

Chance smiled at them, her amber eyes identical to his. Not so long ago, he'd thought she was a threat to his family, accused her of being a spy and worse. He'd been ready to kill her, and she was his kin. Batch-cousin, she'd explained. But she was more than that. She was his batch-sister. She'd forgiven him for what had happened. He hadn't forgiven himself.

"Hey," Chance said, her voice soft and a little sad.

"Hey, sis." He mustered a smile. She was worried about Xori, too. He'd been so caught up in his own fears he'd forgotten that he and Vic weren't the only ones affected. "You holding up okay?"

"More or less. I'd like to do something for you. Once we have all the data, I'd like to parse it and try to calculate outcomes. I don't know what information it might give you, but I want to try."

"You don't need to do that." He'd seen what happened when Chance used her unique abilities on large amounts of data. She could do small calculations on the fly, but when she had to crunch a lot of data, it took a toll that not even her nanotech could heal quickly. The headaches and exhaustion from a single session could wipe her out for days.

"I know. But I want to. Is there anything else you can tell me? The more information I have, the better."

He looked over to the blonde. She was large even for a cyborg female, her size dwarfing every human present, women and men alike. Now he could see her up close, she looked familiar. He scanned his databanks quickly. Cyborg. Friend of Kit and Luke's. An ally, but one who hadn't been around for months because she'd been out mining ore in the asteroid belt. "You're Nya, right?"

"That's me. We've never officially met. I was on my way out into the big black while you two were still recovering. I'm headed back out there in a few days, but I wanted to let you know that if this rescue plan requires a heavy mechanic or cannon fodder, I'm game."

"Thank you," he and Vic said at once.

"And now I've made my offer, I'm going to grab some food while you tell Chance all the things you don't want to say in front of me because I'm a stranger." She grinned and turned to Chance. "And thank you for telling me about where I come from. I'm going to go look up the Kallson family before I head out."

"Is she right? Did you not want her to hear what you're going to tell me?" Chance asked, looking a little confused. Created after the wars had ended, and held prisoner in a research lab for most of her life, Chance still struggled with some nuances of social interaction.

"She was," Vic said, then switched over to a private internal channel to explain about Xori's unique abilities and why it needed to be a closely guarded secret.

Erik looked at the three of them and laughed. "One of these days I'm going to hire someone to build a gizmo so I can listen in on these private conversations."

"Sorry. Chance can catch you up later, but it's faster this way."

Erik cocked a blonde brow. "Faster?"

"Yeah. Talking to each other is just another kind of data transfer," Ward tapped his temple. "We're designed to do that efficiently and really damned fast."

"No one ever mentioned that before," Erik sighed. "It's a good thing I have a healthy ego or being around you lot might make a guy feel downright inferior."

Chance laughed and leaned into him. "You're perfect just the way you are."

Their batch-brothers came over next, with Cynder between them like she was a delicate flower and not one of the most dangerous beings on the station. Toro looking like he was ready to punch through the hull plating, and Ward knew exactly how he felt.

"When you go, your brothers are going with you," Cyn stated, her words bordering on an order.

"No, we're not. We want to, but…" Toro looked at his pregnant wife and shook his head.

"Sorry, Cyn, you're stuck with them," Ward said.

"What if this is a ploy? A distraction to peel off some of us so that you and the sprites are vulnerable?" Vic pointed out. Zura's twins were, for now, the only two children in existence born with their mother's medibots already in their system. Cynder's child would be the third.

"You've been talking to these two behind my back, haven't you?" Cynder demanded.

"Nope. Been a little busy for that, but you're family, Cyn. They stay with you."

"I'd like to go on record as being against this. You're family, too. You need backup," she said.

"They've got it." A new voice joined the conversation.

"In triplicate." Blade and Lance stepped into view, followed by their brother. Dirk, who uttered the last phrase as he came to stand in front of them.

"We have a little experience dealing with members of the Gray's messing with the women we love," Lance said, his voice full of steel.

Ward didn't know what to say. Of everyone here, he'd never expected the triplets to offer to help. Not after what he'd done.

"You three?" Vic said, not bothering to hide his surprise.

"Us three," Lance confirmed.

"And Alyson is okay with it?" Ward asked.

Blade grinned. "She said, and I quote, "kick their saggy gray asses to the other side of the galaxy and bring our friend home.""

Everyone laughed, and the warmth it brought lasted after the laughter faded. "It would be an honor to have you with us."

Vic nodded and soon there were handshakes and shoulder slaps, and then Ward was getting an unexpected hug from Cynder that nearly cracked a rib and his composure.

"Bring her back safe. And don't get cocky. Or dead."

"I'll do my best." But he'd also do whatever it took to ensure Xori and Vic had a long, happy life together.

CHAPTER ELEVEN

THE SHUTTLE TOUCHED down with a bone-jarring bump that made the whole fuselage shudder around her. Whatever abilities the clone at the helm had been programmed with, advanced piloting skills clearly wasn't one of them. Still, they were here. Wherever here was. Xori had tried to engage Five in further conversation, but his answers had been monosyllabic for the most part, and she hadn't wanted to press too hard. She somehow doubted that asking too many questions would be enough to get her spaced, but why take that chance?

Two appeared at the cockpit door and Five stood, gesturing for her to do the same. She'd met Two briefly, when her guard had needed to use the facilities and the second clone had stepped out to keep an eye on her. The fact they never left her alone made her wonder if there was more she could have done, but after several long, boring hours with nothing to do but try to think of a way to save herself, she hadn't come up with anything. Either they were being overcautious, or she'd missed something.

She got to her feet, stretched slowly and carefully, and then fell in between her two guards as they escorted her off the shuttle and into the shuttle bay of a much larger vessel. There were abbreviated notations and what looked like warnings in bright red letters stenciled on the walls of the hangar, but she was too far away to read them. The only thing she could make out was a word painted over a pair of heavy double doors at one end - *Enigma 4.*

She pointed to the doors. "Is that the name of this vessel?"

Neither male answered. Instead, a woman replied. "Yes, it is. Welcome aboard, Dr. Virness."

Xori nearly jumped out of her skin. She spun and came face-to-face with Vivian, who stood only a meter behind her. "I didn't see you there!"

"That is because I was not there to be seen."

It took Xori a second to gather her scattered brain cells into something that worked on more than a primal level. Then she saw what the other female meant. "You're a hologram."

Vivian inclined her head. The motion was somehow more graceful than she'd managed in their video chat. "Sometimes."

"So, when I spoke to you before, on the monitor? That was a holographic projection?"

"No. That was me, in the flesh, as it were." Vivian gestured to the double doors. "Come with me, please.

We have a few things to discuss before we finalize your employment, and I imagine you would like something to eat and drink. The sedative used to incapacitate you has a tendency to cause dehydration."

"Water would be nice, thank you." She followed dutifully along behind Vivian, trying not to stare at the other female's feet. Weirdly enough, the hologram took normal steps even though she moved forward in a gliding motion. The effect was disturbing and a little surreal. Something about it niggled at the back of her brain, but she was too tired and keyed up to think clearly at the moment.

Vivian kept up a running commentary about the ship as they walked, explaining its basic layout and identifying each section as they passed through it. Crew quarters. The galley and mess. Vivian even pointed out the escape pods, and then turned and informed Xori that the pods were not only locked, but set with an explosive that would detonate if they were activated without the proper codes being entered. Her tone never changed, and she went back to discussing the ship's amenities as if booby-trapped escape pods were of no more import than the wide array of options programmed into the food dispensers. It was even more unnerving than her holographic glide step, but not as strange as seeing the same two faces again and again. Males who were identical to her guards, and a single type of female clone, all with golden skin, dark hair, and heart-shaped faces. Vivian didn't pay them any attention, moving past them as if they didn't exist, and they did the same, their gazes fixed on some point behind Xori and her little group as if they weren't there at all.

They eventually stopped outside a door marked with her name in a sharp white print that seemed similar to her office back on Astek station. She looked again and realized it was *exactly* the same. Same size. Same font. Same spacing. A chill crept down her spine. "How long were you spying on me?"

"Since the moment you were brought in to treat the subjects of our Reaper project."

Which meant that all her patients, their friends and family, had been under surveillance far longer than any of them had guessed.

"If you would place your hand on the scanner, please?" Vivian pointed to the access pad beside the door.

She did so. There was a low hum, a beep, and the door slid open.

"Your biometrics are now verified and loaded into the ship's system. If a door opens when you stand in front of it, you are permitted to enter. If a door remains closed, you do not. Do you understand?"

"Yes." She got the message loud and clear.

"Good. Then our tour is complete. Welcome home, Dr. Virness. These quarters are yours until we reach our final destination."

"Do I get to know where that is?" She didn't expect to be granted that information, but she felt the need to ask, anyway.

Then she stepped inside her new rooms. It was a standard shipboard layout, though somewhat larger than she was used to. There was a small sitting area, a food dispenser so basic it likely only produced beverages, a workspace, and a small bed. What furniture she saw was simple but comfortable looking. There was a single viewport in one wall, or maybe it was just a monitor made to look like a viewport. She was so turned around after her tour she had no idea how close they were to the hull at the moment.

Vivian glided in behind her. "Where? No. But I can tell you *what* it is. This ship is one of many. They are small-scale laboratories and means of transportation. We also have a main research station. That is our destination, once I have determined we are not being followed."

Xori felt a spark of hope. Followed? Did Vivian think there was a chance her males were coming to rescue her? She kept her expression neutral and continued to explore the area. There was a small sanitation cubby through a door near the bed, but otherwise, there wasn't much else to see. The furniture was all too heavy to move, and she noted with mild amusement that there was nothing she could use as even the most rudimentary of weapons. She looked closer, running her hand over the corner of the desk. No corners. No edges.

The display above the desk was an interactive hologram with no monitor or means of connecting to the system directly. It was likely a dummy terminal. She glanced at the data on the digital screen, froze, and leaned in to take a closer look. "These are my work files. My private, encrypted files about my patients."

"Yes, they are. Though as you can see, they are no longer encrypted. I told you, Dr. Virness. We have been watching you for quite some time. Your assessments of our previous projects have already proven helpful. As I am sure you have heard, we have lost a number of personnel and test subjects lately. Your recruitment will help us refill our ranks."

"You used my notes to improve your process?" Bile curdled in her stomach. She had been working to undo the damage this group had done, and they were using her insights to inflict more harm on others.

"We did. We always intended to recruit you eventually, but when we discovered your other abilities, we advanced our timetable."

"Other abilities?" *Veth*. They knew.

"You are a powerful empath, Dr. Virness. I have viewed the footage. I saw what you did to the Reaper you call Ward. That is the reason you are here, now."

"You want me to read the emotions of the clones and cyborgs you've created, and assess if any of them are breaking their conditioning."

"Yes. And much more. You are an invaluable tool, Dr. Virness, and we intend to use you to your full potential." The hologram gestured to the males standing by the door. "Before we get to that, though. There's one other thing we need to accomplish. Two, Five, please secure the doctor for the procedure."

"What procedure?" Xori's voice was tight with fear and she backed away from the clones.

"Please, don't resist. It won't do you any good."

She looked around in panic, even though she

already knew there was nowhere to run and nothing she could use to protect herself. "Tell me what you're going to do!"

Vivian extended her hand. Cupped in her palm was a small, oblong object. "I believe you can guess what this is?"

Xori stared in horror. She had a good idea what it was, and the thought of having one of those inside her body was horrifying. "It's one of those chips you implant into beings."

"It is. It will allow us to monitor your location at all times."

"And if you activate the micro-explosive inside, I die." She'd heard about these from Nyx.

Vivian closed her hand. "Yes, you will."

A male pointed to a chair. "Sit."

She swallowed hard and fought the urge to look at the door again. There was no way she'd reach it, and if she did, there wasn't a soul on this entire ship who'd lift a finger to help her. She sat.

"Thank you for being sensible. I assure you, this is a safe and only mildly uncomfortable procedure, and after it is done, we will leave you alone to rest." Vivian glanced at the door into the corridor. It slid open without her saying a word, and a female entered. She was dressed in the same nondescript off-white jumpsuits as the other clones she'd seen since coming aboard.

Xori spotted the injector she carried and had to fight back another surge of panic.

Vivian was either ignoring her fear or didn't notice it

and proceeded to an oddly formal introduction. "Dr. Virness, this is Beta. She will be performing the procedure. I am also assigning her as your personal assistant. She will see to it that you have everything you need and act as your guide both here, and after you are transferred to the main research station."

The female looked exactly like every other one she'd seen. "And how will I be able to tell her apart from the others?"

Vivian's face went blank. As if the thought hadn't occurred to her. "That is not something I had considered, but I believe I have a solution. Beta will attire herself in blue from now on. That will allow you to identify her."

"Uh, thank you."

"You will find that we can be quite reasonable, Dr. Virness. Despite what you have been told, we are not monsters."

Says the female who threatened to throw me out an airlock if I caused problems and is about to stick an explosive in my neck. If she got out of this alive, she'd need to book some time in her own sim program to get some payback on the Ariel Coal hologram. Maybe Vic and Ward could help. Group therapy.

She closed her eyes as the female clone moved around behind her. When the injector touched the side of her neck, she conjured up memories of Vic and Ward. The laughter and happiness she'd found on their first date. The heat of their kisses, the way they caressed her with such tenderness and passion. She held those thoughts close to her heart, repeating their names over and over. For a second, they almost felt real, their presence a comfort even if it wasn't real.

I waited too long. If I'd said yes sooner, we could have had more time together. Made more memories.

As the injector hissed and the pain came, she made herself a promise. If she ever saw them again, she'd finish what she'd started. She would tell the galaxy she'd made her choice and let the chips fall where they may. Life was too short for anything else.

It took less than an hour for Corp-Sec and Nova Force to combine forces and retrieve the missing security footage from secret data caches put in place for just this kind of thing. Vic didn't know if it was good planning or paranoia that the backups existed at all, but he was grateful they did. Xori's abduction had been recorded, her attacker's face loaded into every database they could think of looking for a match, and they had the name and transponder code of the shuttle she'd been taken aboard. After that, things had happened with head-spinning speed.

Nyx had viewed the footage and recognized the man as someone she'd killed escaping from the Gray Men. If the original was dead, then this one had to be a clone. None of the military people present reacted with surprise to the news the Grays were involved in illegal cloning, but it hit the rest of them hard. There were no depths these assholes wouldn't sink to, and now, they were operating on the station openly instead of using go-betweens to do their dirty work. They'd hired bounty-hunters to go after Chance, but this time, they'd sent their own people. Things were escalating fast, and that was bad news for everyone.

Once Archer had confirmation the Grays were involved, he and the Nova Force members present pushed to take over the mission. That wasn't going to happen. Vic had left Ward arguing with Archer and stepped out into the corridor to calm down before he did something regrettable, like throw the by-the-book colonel through a bulkhead. He couldn't think clearly about any of this, not when Xori's life was on the line. He needed her to be alright.

He scoffed at himself. It was so much more than that. He needed her, period.

"You look like you could use some good news," a deep rumbling voice intruded on his moment of peace. Denz had followed him out, and the big male's black eyes were full of sympathy.

"I could. You got any to spare?"

Denz held up a massive fist. "As a matter of fact, I do." He turned his hand over and opened it, revealing an unmarked injector vial.

"What's that?"

"Something that might help you bring the doctor back in one piece." Denz lowered his voice. "Take it, and do not, under any circumstances, let Archer know you have that."

Vic slipped the vial into his pocket, feeling like he was taking part in some sort of illicit deal. "What is it?"

"The next generation of medi-bots. Before he died,

Zale was teaching me about nanotech. He wanted to be sure that someone outside the IAF knew how to make them, in case the military tried to close that door again."

Vic dropped a hand to his pocket, suddenly aware of how valuable the simple object was. Zale had been one of the original creators of the nanotech that every cyborg carried. After the war, he'd created a version that could be safely injected into anyone, cyborg or not. The IAF had confiscated the tech, but not before the little crew of rebels at the Nova had inoculated all the non-cyborgs in their circle.

"It's safe for a Pheran?"

Denz nodded. "It is. I took all of Zale's notes with me to the colony and shared it with the Vardarians. They use nanotech, too, even more than we do. That vial contains the new and improved version we figured out between us."

"Thank you." The words weren't nearly enough to express his gratitude. If they found Xori – no, *when* they found her—dosing her with this would permanently accelerate and enhance her ability to heal, increase her physical endurance, and ensure that she lived just as long as they did.

"Zale wanted to protect everyone in this crazy crew. This is my way of carrying on his legacy. I left a few more doses with Dr. Jeffries. She'll see to it they get used the way Zale would have wanted."

"It's not just Zale's legacy anymore. It's yours, too." He clapped Denz on the shoulder, vaguely amused by the fact he had to reach *up* to it. Cyborgs were taller than most of the other species, but with his mix of

Torski and human genes, Denz was close to two-and-a-half meters tall.

Denz chuckled. "Maybe." The big male tapped his fist lightly to Vic's bicep. "See you back inside."

Vic let Ward know he would be back soon and headed for their quarters. The little vial in his pocket was a symbol of hope. They'd get Xori back. They'd inject her with the nanotech so she'd be healthy and safe, and then he'd tell her all the things he held in his heart. But as much as he wanted to hold onto it, he needed to stash that in his bag before he came anywhere near Archer again.

Nothing would stop him from giving it to Xori. Not Archer. Not the Gray Men. No one.

Once they were on their way, Vic expected to feel better. He didn't. If anything, he felt worse. There was nothing to do but think, pace, and go through all the ways he was going to hurt the ones who had tried to take Xori away from them.

Tink was piloting the *Faerie Queene,* and despite the fact they had special permission to exceed all speed restrictions near the collection of stations that formed the Drift, it would still take time to catch up with Xori. If the vessel Chance predicted she was on didn't move before they got there. If they'd tracked the right shuttle. If Chance's projections were right. If. If. If.

He paced the length of the ship, too wound up to sit still for long. Ward was doing the same thing, and they'd pass each other somewhere around the midpoint every five minutes or so. It would have been funny if the situation wasn't so dire.

Thoughts of Xori filled his head. Was she alright? Was she hurt? Afraid? His thoughts chased after each other in obsessive circles. He was so caught up in them that the first time he heard her voice, he thought it was just his mind playing tricks on him.

The second time he heard her, he wasn't so sure. She spoke his name, as calmly as if she had just walked up behind him. For one brief moment, he felt her presence, a subtle disturbance in the air, a hint of her scent. He whirled around, but the corridor was empty.

He checked his onboard systems, but they hadn't detected anything. No sound. No one else around. As real as it felt, it had to have been in his head, but had felt so *real*.

"This is no time to start losing your damned mind," he muttered to himself, then turned and went back to pacing.

When he crossed paths with Ward this time, a door opened and all three Trello brothers piled into the hall, blocking their path. "You two are wearing a hole in Tianna's very expensive new carpet," Blade pointed out.

Ward growled. It was a wordless sound thick with frustration.

Lance grinned and growled back.

Ward blinked, then shook his head and barked out a grudging laugh. "You're a lunatic."

"I thought that was common knowledge," Lance replied.

Dirk sighed and looked at Vic with an expression that said 'and this is what I have to deal with all day,' as clearly as if he'd spoken the words out loud.

He nodded back, and something uncoiled a little deep in his chest. "Tell me about it."

"Instead of pacing, you two want to go over the plan again?" Dirk jerked his head toward the door they'd come out of. "Tink told us to use this place as a command center."

"Talking about it is the next best thing to actually doing it," Blade chimed in.

"Yeah. We should go over it again," Vic agreed.

"When are we going to tell the Nova Force team about the change in plans?" Blade asked as they all filed inside.

"We figure thirty seconds before we implement it should be about right. Give them a small window to yell at us before we ignore them and do it, anyway. That way, it looks like they at least tried to stop us," Ward said, dropping into one of the couches that lined one wall. It was more a lounge than a meeting room, but there was a table with a built-in data display that would work for working out the details. Not that they had many.

Officially, they were here to back up Commander Dax Rossi and his team. At least, that was the agreement they'd made with Colonel Archer. The thing was, the *Faerie Queene* was fast. Even using only her standard engines, she'd been gradually pulling ahead of Rossi's ship since they'd left the station. By the time they got to Xori, they'd have ten minutes to put their plan in motion before the other ship could catch them.

Vic was pretty sure the *Malora's* crew was expecting them to go their own way. Nothing had been said aloud, but Lt. Caldwell, the Nova Force medic, and coincidentally, Alyson's older brother, had quietly given Ward a scanner for detecting the chips the Grays were fond of. He'd also given them a device he promised could temporarily block any attempts to trigger the explosive. The thought of Xori being alone out there with a *fraxxing* micro-explosive in her body made him want to scream and rail at the universe. It was also the reason they weren't trying to put any more distance between them and the *Malora*. If she did have one of the chips, there was no way they'd be able to remove it themselves. For that, they'd need Caldwell and a military-grade med-bay.

Vic picked a seat near Ward, and they all started talking through the plan from the beginning. As they talked, his brother sent him a private message. *"We're going to get her back."*

"Yes, we will." They had to, because he couldn't imagine a future for them that didn't include her.

CHAPTER TWELVE

THEY'RE HERE. She couldn't say exactly how she knew. It was barely a whisper of breath against her awareness. Like a trace of a favorite scent in the air, here and gone before she could be sure she'd sensed it at all, but somehow, she knew what it meant. Vic and Ward had come for her.

The time had passed with painful slowness, and every moment she'd expected to hear the rumble of the ship's FTL drive coming online. Once that happened, her odds of escaping would plummet, and she'd be left with only two choices: cooperate and live, or refuse and die. She'd done her best not to think that far ahead, and focused on the here and now, instead.

She'd showered and changed into one of the unflattering jumpsuits she found folded in a drawer. Beta had brought her something to eat, and she'd spent the rest of her time reviewing the documentation Vivian had provided. Page after page of experiments, most of them deemed failures and terminated, including the Reaper and Fury projects. She knew beings who'd been part of those *failures*, and as she pored over the dry, scientific summaries of what had been done to Ward, Victor, and Nyx, she questioned how any being could choose to inflict this kind of harm on any other.

Once she sensed their arrival, she rose from the desk and went to stand by the viewport, as if she'd be able to spot their ship out there in the impossibly vast expanse. She didn't question her feelings. It didn't matter that it shouldn't be possible. It was. She was sure of it. Her *vardo* had found her.

She paused and replayed her last thought. *Vardo*? Was that what they were to her? Her mates? She stared out past her dim reflection to the sea of stars beyond and the answer came to her quietly, another whisper from the depths of her soul. *Yes.*

Regret gnawed at her with needle-sharp teeth. How had she missed it? Why hadn't she seen the truth of it until now? She shook herself, casting the dark thoughts aside. How and why didn't matter. She couldn't change the past. All she could do was be smarter here in the present and hope they had a future to look forward to.

A second later everything erupted into chaos. There was a distant sound like thunder, the lights flickered, and the ship shuddered so hard beneath her feet she had to grab the edges of the viewport to keep her balance. Her senses were still scrambled from what she assumed was some kind of attack when a klaxon tore through the air, a tri-tone alert that repeated twice, and died away only to be replaced by a reddish cast to the lights, which started to strobe to the same triple beat as the alarm. *Definitely an attack*, then.

The door to her room slid open only seconds later. She turned, half expecting to see Vic or Ward appear, even though she knew that wasn't likely.

It wasn't them, of course. It was Beta. She must have been standing outside in case Xori called for her.

There were lines of worry around the female's mouth and her eyes were wide, the whites showing more than usual. "You need to come with me immediately. We are being boarded by raiders. I've been instructed to get you safely to a shuttle. This ship is running with a minimal crew compliment and may not be able to repel a boarding party."

"Of course." She tried to look scared as she hurried to join the other woman. As if she were terrified of the thought of raiders and not elated that her rescue was at hand. "Is there a way I can bring the data I was looking at with me? I'd already made some notes."

Beta crossed over to the work area and pulled a data stick out of the top drawer. She reached into the holographic display with the stick and the entire image flowed into the object like water flowing into a drain. She'd never seen anything like it.

"Your notes." Beta handed her the data stick as she moved past her, clearly eager to get going.

They were close enough Xori could sense the female's anxiety. It surprised her to realize that Beta actually believed what she'd said about being attacked by raiders. There were none of the usual signs of duplicity, only a nearly compulsive need to get to safety.

It had to be something to do with the clone's behavioral conditioning.

Xori considered quickly as she followed along behind Beta. She couldn't do anything about the compulsion, but the anxiousness? That, she could work with.

They moved through the corridors, occasionally pressing themselves up against a wall as the male clones ran back and forth, all of them wearing combat armor and bristling with weapons. Beta's emotions were stronger now, her anxiety growing teeth and claws as it morphed into fear. Xori did what she could to amplify that. It wasn't easy, given they weren't in physical contact, but it was easier than stripping away Ward's anger. This time, she was fanning the flames of a fire that was already burning.

"Hurry. We're almost there." Beta's voice was high and frantic as she pointed to a set of double doors with a shaking finger.

Xori felt a pang of guilt, but it didn't stop her from pushing another wave of fear into her guide. If she got onto that shuttle, she'd never see her *vardo* again.

Footsteps rushed up behind her, and she barely managed to dive out of the way as three of the males ran by them without a word of warning. They were going flat out, weapons in hand.

One of them clipped Beta, who tumbled to the deck with a fearful cry and stayed down, her knees drawn up to her chest and her hands over her head.

Xori didn't stop to see if she was alright. This was her chance. She started running after the three males.

They were clearly preparing to defend the ship from the alleged raiders Beta had mentioned, the ones she was certain were really her rescue party. She was going to need help to get off this nightmare ship, but she could at least make it easy for them to find her.

To her surprise, she didn't have to run far. The males she was following made straight for the same double doors Beta had pointed out. They charged into the shuttle hangar shoulder to shoulder, weapons firing. Xori took cover on one side of the door. She had no weapon, no armor, and no idea what was going on inside. She'd be safer out here. *Maybe.* Or Beta might snap out of it and drag her away, or Vivian could show up, or—the doors started to close again, and she dashed through them before she finished her thought. Vic and Ward were on the other side of that door. They had to be. It wasn't rational or even smart, but she was done playing things safe. It was time for a leap of faith.

Ward stood at the edge of the airlock and eyed the distance from their ship to their target. "This idea seemed a lot less insane when we were running simulations."

Blade's voice came through his helmet with such clarity it was like he was standing right next to him. "That's the problem with reality. It's too *fraxxing* real."

"And these suits are very fraxxing *tight,"* Vic muttered on their internal channel.

"Self-tailoring nanotech or not, I don't think these were

designed with cyborgs in mind," Ward agreed. But they were thin enough they could wear combat armor overtop. It was a decent trade-off for the reduced blood flow and uncomfortable fit.

They were in the airlock, waiting to move the second they got close enough. To the surprise of no one who knew the owners, the Faerie Queene was outfitted with military-grade weaponry and stealth abilities that made her a match for half the ships in the IAF's fleets. They'd managed to sneak up on their target undetected, and by the time the other ship's engines had been crippled by a perfectly placed plasma cannon round, he and Vic were suited up and prepared for the next stage of their assault.

"You ready to go get our girl?" Vic asked over the main channel,

"Locked and loaded. Just don't drop our guns. We're going to need those."

Blade's voice filled his helmet again. "Kick their asses for us."

"Will do," Vic replied.

"We're in position. You are good to go in three. Three-two-one-mark."

They pushed off the moment Blade gave the word, activating their suit's simple thrusters the second they hit open space. Around them, the void filled with bolts from the plasma cannon, and the skin on the back of Ward's neck tightened as the other vessel returned fire. The light show had two purposes, to take out the other vessel's weapons, and draw everyone's attention away from them so they could make it to the other ship undetected.

"One nice thing. If they *fraxx* up and hit us with one of those bolts, we'll never even feel it." Vic said.

"I'm not going to shoot you." Blade stated, sounding vaguely insulted.

Two heartbeats later, a plasma bolt streaked past just over their heads. "Oops," Blade said a half-second after that.

"Asshole," Ward muttered. He knew there wasn't any real risk of getting taken out by friendly fire. He'd reviewed the calculations himself. Twice.

They dropped below the plane of the firefight and soared across the open space, as he did his best to stay focused on the fast-approaching hull of the ship. The plan was to skim beneath the ship's belly and gain access through the shuttle hangar on the far side. Chance had predicted it would have the outer doors open in preparation for an emergency evac using the shuttle docked there. She'd also told them the ship was likely called the Enigma and sure enough that was the name emblazoned on her hull. The *Enigma 4*. He had no idea how she could have known that, but now he had confirmation he was confident she'd nailed the rest of her projections, too.

They passed so close to the other ship he could have reached out and touched her hull. Not that it would be a good idea. Out here in the void, any contact he made would alter his trajectory, and they'd need most of the nitrogen propellant their suits used to change direction and reach their target. If they ran out before they killed their momentum, they'd fly right past the ship and out into space with no way back. The thought of dying didn't bother him, but taking his last breath out here, alone in the dark was not the way he wanted to go.

"Turn and burn coming up," Vic said.

Ward checked his own instruments, confirmed, and tried not to tense up as the seconds ticked away. He hated this next part. They activated their suits' prepared program at the same time, and the onboard computer took over, sending out a jet of nitrogen gas to slow them, before setting off another series of carefully calculated thruster spurts that spun them one-hundred-eighty degrees so they could see the *Enigma* again.

The sudden deceleration was unpleasant, and the spinning made him nauseous, but at least it was over quickly. They sailed the last few meters to the other ship, and he managed to slap a magnetized glove onto the hull with Vic less than a meter above him.

"Low gravity was a lot more fun when we were naked and had Xori with us," Vic grumbled.

Ward grinned. Not just at the memory, but because his brother had just made that comment over the main channel.

A chorus of laughter and groans filled his helmet and one of the triplets choked out, "That is more than we ever needed to know about your sex life."

Ward ignored the noise and leaned over to get his first look at the shuttle bay. The doors were open, and he could see the heavy shimmer of a force field over the opening. It was designed to allow shuttles to come and go without losing the atmosphere. He couldn't make out much except that there was definitely a shuttle present, and the area was bathed in the strobing red light of an alert. He hoped whoever was onboard was focused on the *Faerie Queene*'s attack and hadn't spotted them making the crossing. If there was an ambush waiting inside, this was going to be a very short mission.

He unslung his rifle and pressed the butt of it against the energy shield. There was some resistance, but with a little more pressure, it passed through with no apparent harm.

He was about to tell Vic they were good to go when he felt it, a gossamer whisper of *something* that felt like Xori. It was gone a second later, but it left him with a sense of renewed urgency.

"She's close," Vic said over their private link.

"You felt it, too?"

"Yeah. I thought I did once before, too. But…"

Ward nodded. It was an ingrained habit that was useless since Vic couldn't see the movement from their current positions. *"Me too."* He'd thought he'd imagined it the last time, but now, he knew better. She was waiting for them somewhere close.

"We'll have to ask her how she did that when we see her again." Vic pulled a blaster from its holster, checked the readout, then signaled he was ready to go.

Ward shifted his body along the hull, getting into position. "See you on the other side. Expect a little resistance going in."

"That's what she said," one of the triplets joked, then yelped in startled pain.

"My brother is an idiot. Apologies."

A new voice cut into the chatter. "For the love of gravity, enough joking around. Frankly, it's a *fraxxing* miracle you've all survived this long. This is Commander Rossi on the *Malora*. Sit-rep, please."

Vic started to give an update, but Ward didn't wait. He stuck a hand through the field, grabbed onto the edge of the hull, and pulled himself inside.

Vic stopped talking and swung in behind him, both of them falling to the deck as they crossed into the artificial gravity field inside the ship.

He hit, rolled, and was back on his feet and moving before his brain caught up to his body. He scanned the area for potential threats, but didn't see anything but the powered-down shuttle. He shouldered his weapon, unlatched his helmet and tossed it to Vic, who shoved it into the container that held most of their weapons. Their exit plans didn't require helmets, but there was no sense leaving anything behind.

Ward tapped his throat mic to activate it while Vic handed him the rest of his arsenal and then shot out every security camera he could find. "We're in. No contact yet. How's it looking out there?"

"This is Dirk. The *Malora* is coming into position now. The Enigma's engines are still offline and we've done enough damage to her weapon system she's not shooting back anymore. We're going to hold here while Rossi's team breaches their airlock and boards."

Command Rossi spoke next. "Confirmed. We'll join the party as soon as we can." He didn't add 'since you two idiots charged on ahead without us,' but it was definitely implied.

He rolled his shoulders and settled his rifle into a more comfortable grip, listening in as Vic coordinated the details with the other teams. It wouldn't be long before their presence was discovered, and once that happened, all hell would break loose.

They were on their way to the only cover in the hangar – the shuttle – never taking their eyes off the only exit. "You know, this is the first time in our lives we've gone into a battle for something we wanted, and not as someone else's pawn," Vic said.

Ward nodded. Felt the rightness of the moment. Grinned at his brother. "This is our choice. Feels good, doesn't it?"

"Yeah, it really does."

A thought stirred in the back of his mind, something about Xori and choices, but before it could fully form, three identical men charged into the hangar and started shooting, the shots slamming into the shuttle's hull.

"Son of a bitch, they know where we are," Vic snarled as he returned fire, then ducked back behind cover.

"Looks like you missed a cam—" the rest of the sentence died unspoken as he spotted a familiar figure darting through the doors behind the others. Slender, graceful, and an unmistakable shade of blue. *Xori.*

He couldn't speak past the lump of fear that clotted in his throat, so he switched to their internal channel. *"Xori's in here. We need to clear this room, right* fraxxing *now."*

Vic didn't answer, he just charged out into the open with a war cry that Ward hadn't heard in years. He followed a few steps behind, screaming his own battle cry. The fight was over before the echoes faded, Then he was racing to where Xori was hunched down beside a small stack of cargo crates. It was only partial cover, and she was curled into such a tight ball he couldn't tell if she was hiding or injured.

"Are you hurt?" He called as he ran to her, shoving his rifle back over his shoulder so his hands were free.

She looked up and managed a grim little smile. "Just terrified."

She rose on shaky legs and crossed the last meter at a run, hitting him with surprising force and wrapping her arms around his waist with a sob of relief. "You came."

He crushed her to him as tight as he dared, lowering his head so he could brush his lips over her hair. "Of course we did. You're ours, Xori. No one will ever take you away from us." The words hit him like a hammer blow, shattering the last of his walls. The truth dawned, bringing darkness to the deepest parts of his soul. He hadn't come after her to make sure she had a life with Vic. He'd was here because he needed her, too.

"Get her to cover, I'll deal with these assholes." Vic was kicking weapons away from their opponents and ensuring they were well and truly dead in the most efficient way possible - a blaster bolt to the head.

When the first shot fired, Xori looked toward the sound, but Ward turned her so she couldn't see what

Vic was doing. He didn't want her exposed to anything that ugly. "Eyes on me, little star."

She looked up at him, her silver eyes bright with an almost manic energy.

"I knew that if I followed those males, I'd find you."

"You…" He groaned. "You went looking for trouble because you thought we'd be in the middle of it? What if you'd gotten hurt?"

She blinked, then jerked away from him with panic in her eyes. "Hurt? *Veth*! Let me go! I'm dangerous." She pointed to her neck. "There's a chip. A bomb. You both need to stay back. I don't know how big the blast radius is."

Fraxx, he'd been so eager to get to her he'd forgotten one of the mission parameters. He pulled the device Lt. Caldwell had given him out of the protective pouch at his waist, activated it, and shoved it into her hands. "Hold this. Do not let go. Do you understand? If you drop this, you die. It will block any signal they try to send to the chip."

She nodded once. "You knew they'd do this to me?"

"We didn't. Nova Force did. They're here, too." He tugged her into his arms and kissed her hard. It was a foolish risk, but the armor and vac-suit put too many layers between them, and he needed to feel her touch, even if it was only for a moment. He had to be sure she was really here.

Xori moaned and rose on her toes, her arms twining around his neck as she kissed him back with equal fervor, mouth parting, tongue twining with his. He cradled her close, his fingers tangling in her hair even though he couldn't feel it through his gloves. She was sweet, and warm, and real, and his world was a little lighter just because she was near him.

The too-small suit suddenly shrank another three sizes as a wave of need crashed over him, firing up the most primal parts of his brain. He wanted to throw her over his shoulder and carry her off to somewhere safe. Then tear off her clothes and make love to her for a week.

"Hold that thought," He murmured against her lips when sanity returned enough for him to remember where they were.

"And the blocker thingy," she said, holding up the hand still gripping the device he'd handed her.

"And that." He swung her into his arms and ran back to the shuttle, painfully aware that she had no protection from incoming fire. The shapeless gray shipsuit she wore wouldn't stop a sneeze, never mind a blaster bolt.

Vic made it there ahead of him, almost tearing Xori out of his hold the moment they got close. He kissed her hard, and Ward grinned as he recognized the same burning need for her that he'd felt.

"What the *fraxx* are you doing here, blossom?" Vic demanded when he came up for air.

"Looking for you. I figured this was faster than waiting to be rescued."

Vic made the same strangled groaning noise that Ward had. "You…"

"I know," Ward agreed. "We'll have to discuss that, later."

The doors opened again and another wave of identical men charged through. "How many of these clones are there?" Vic growled in frustration as he returned fire.

"Fifteen." Xori replied.

"What?" both he and Vic asked at once. "How can you be sure?"

"Because I asked."

"And they told you?" Vic's incredulity matched his own.

"Well, yes. I'm very easy to talk to." Xori's voice was bright and brittle.

He ducked back into cover to check on her. She was standing behind them, arms wrapped around herself, her lips turned up in a tight, adrenaline-fueled smile.

"What else can you tell us?"

Her brow creased, and he guessed she was trying to think clearly. Not an easy thing to do while being shot at. "Oh! Vivian!"

"One sec." He leaned out and picked off another of their attackers. They had no cover, which made it easier than it could have been.

"Vivian is—" The rest of what she said was eclipsed by a piercing alert.

"Decompression warning! Shuttle or doors?" Vic asked via their internal channel.

"Shuttle would be smarter."

He dropped the last of the clones and turned back to Xori. "That's a decompression alarm. Come on, we have to get inside the shuttle." The words were barely out of his mouth when something shimmered into existence right behind Xori. It took him a split second to recognize her face, and another to get over the shock. Ariel *fraxxing* Coal.

His first instinct was to lunge for her, to shoot her, or scream. But he'd already faced this demon once before. This time, it was easier to control his reaction.

Vic cursed and raised his pulse rifle, then stopped and lowered it again. "Just a distraction," he muttered.

"Hardly." The projection spoke in Ariel's voice a moment after the alarm cut off, leaving the shuttle bay eerily quiet.

That…probably wasn't a good thing. He ignored the Ariel hologram and reached out to Xori. "Come on, we're leaving."

The hologram vanished, but almost immediately it spoke again, this time from behind him. "You're not going anywhere, Reaper."

He and Victor spun around, putting themselves between Xori and this weird new threat.

"Vivian, stop this. Please." Xori pleaded. "I'll cooperate, but not if you kill them. Stop the decompression cycle and let them go. The Reaper project failed. You don't need them. You need me to stop that happening again."

"It's stopped. I just wanted to get your attention." The hologram held up a device that looked identical to the one he'd given Xori. "Since my first attempt to end this little standoff didn't go as planned."

Xori gasped and looked at her hand. The signal blocker was flashing an angry red. "You tried to kill me?"

"You think I wouldn't? You're only valuable to us if you're willing to cooperate. Otherwise…" Ariel, or Vivian, whatever she was calling herself now, shrugged. "I'm starting to believe the only way to get that from you is through incentive. Of course, I only need one of them for that."

There was a brief silence, and that's when he heard it: a single footfall from behind them. *Fraxxing* hell, the hologram had managed to distract them after all.

CHAPTER THIRTEEN

Xori's thoughts were racing almost as fast as her heart. She'd only just found them, and now she might lose them again – forever, this time.

Danger and fear sharpened all her senses, including her psychic ones. She'd felt the presence of the male coming up behind her before she heard him, and she spun around at the same moment he rounded the side of the shuttle. Vic and Ward both cried out, and she knew what would happen if she didn't act before they did. Ward would lay down his life for her because he didn't believe he was worthy, and Vic would protect them both, no matter what the cost. She couldn't let that happen.

She ran straight for the male with a feral howl she didn't know she was capable of making, anger boiling up from deep inside her. She'd spent too many years submitting meekly, apologizing for any slight, real or imagined. She'd gotten so good at avoiding conflict she'd left her homeworld to escape it. Yet, here she was again, being threatened and bullied by beings who wanted to control her and make her submit.

No more.

She bared her teeth, her talon-tipped fingers curving into claws as she ran. She reached out with her gifts without even being sure what she could do, but knowing she had to do *something*. All the rage, pain, and fear she felt flowed out of her in a dizzying wave.

The male raised his gun, fired, and her perception shifted and slowed, her life passing in a series of disjointed images. She was running. Then there was a light tap on her shoulder. The next moment she was falling, and the floor rushed up to meet her. Someone was screaming. It sounded terrible. Ragged. Agonized. She hoped it wasn't her. The floor was closer now. She closed her eyes. *This is going to hurt.*

It didn't. For all she could tell, she might have landed on a cloud of feathers instead of a hard metal deck. She cracked open one eye, saw nothing but darkness, and realized that was because she was face down on the deck. The moment she lifted her head, the pain hit all at once. An ambush of agonies that made her want to scream, or better yet, lose consciousness. Only she couldn't do that.

It took her a second to remember why not. Vivian. Vic and Ward. The male who'd snuck up on them. Danger!

She tried to push herself up, but one arm refused to work and a fresh wave of pain sent her crashing back to the floor with a frustrated cry. Time skipped again, and when she came back to her senses, there was blood in her mouth, and her shoulder felt like it had been dipped in rocket fuel and set on fire.

Boots appeared in her vision, and she blinked at them blearily, trying to guess if they belonged to Ward, Victor, or their attacker. No, it wouldn't be the clone. A fragment of a memory came to her. The male dropping the gun, eyes wide, mouth open impossibly wide as he screamed and crumpled to the ground. Had she done that to him? She thought she might have. She didn't have the energy to feel bad about it. Maybe later.

"Hey, blossom. You still with us?" Gentle hands turned her over, and she looked up into Vic's amber gaze. He was grim-faced with worry that only softened a little when he saw she was awake.

"Still here." Her words came out thick and flat. She reached up to touch her lips. Ow. Bad idea. Her lip was cut, and she suspected her nose was broken, too.

"What the hell were you thinking charging at him like that?"

She started to smile, then winced as even that small movement added new pains to the growing list. "If I hadn't, one of you would have done it instead."

He knocked on his chest plate, knuckles rapping against armor. "Well, yeah, because we came prepared to get shot at."

"Not the point." She lifted her good arm and touched his cheek. "I know you would both make that sacrifice for me without hesitation, but I love you both too much to let either of you do that."

"Is that so?" He leaned down and kissed her softly

on her forehead. "I feel the same way, so how about we make a deal? None of us goes for the sacrifice play, and we all get the hell out of here alive."

"Sounds good. Better tell Ward, though."

"I will. I need to get a look at your shoulder. It's going to hurt. You ready for that?"

She risked a tiny nod. "Can't hurt more than it does already."

He grunted. "I wouldn't bet on that." He placed a gentle hand on her shoulder and then her world filled with pain beyond understanding. A moment later it faded away, along with everything else.

When she came to again, she was in someone's arms. Her mind was foggy, but the pain was less than it had been. Not gone, exactly, but very far away.

"Welcome back. How are you feeling? I dosed you with some powerful pain-blockers, they working, yet?" Vic asked.

"Feeling better." She smiled, and this time it only stung a little. "Drugs must be working."

"Good."

"So good," A memory drifted through her awareness. A male aiming at her. Shooting. Screaming. "Did…did I harm someone back there. Before?"

Vic paused, then nodded slowly. "I don't know what you did, or how, but you put that guy down without laying a finger on him. Ward dealt with him while I was looking after you."

"I think I should feel bad about that. But I don't."

"He doesn't deserve your sympathy, or your regret. He tried to kill you."

There was a distant sound of someone shooting. She flinched and tried to curl up tighter in Vic's arms, but something thick and blocky made it impossible. She moved her good hand down her chest and discovered she'd been wrapped in a piece of body armor. She reached for Vic, pressing a hand to his unprotected chest. "Why am I wearing your armor?"

"To keep you alive."

"But what if they shoot you instead?"

"That's why I'm carrying you. You're my shield."

Even drugged, that didn't sound like a great plan to her, but she was in no position to argue. They ducked into a side corridor as another round of shooting started. "Where's Ward?" she asked.

"Right here, sweetheart. Just clearing a path for us. We're on our way to rendezvous with the others."

He sounded so calm it was easy to forget what his words really meant. He was killing the last of the clones so the three of them could escape. She wondered if Five was still alive. Probably not.

"You happen to know how many female clones were on this ship?" Vic asked.

"No, but they're created in batches of fifteen if that helps," she replied.

"Not a lot of crew on this ship," Someone, she thought it was Ward, said. It was getting hard to think again.

"It's for transport, I think. Mostly. They were taking me to a research station."

She didn't mean to, but she took a little nap after

that, and when she came awake again, they were on the move.

Ward walked beside her now, and when he saw her looking at him, he smiled, then reached down to grab something resting on her stomach. It was the device he'd given her, the one that stopped her chip from exploding. "I thought I told you not to let go of this."

She held out her hand and he placed it gently inside, closed her fingers around it, and squeezed lightly. "We'll discuss your punishment later."

"Punishment?"

"Oh yes. Or did you think we were going to overlook the fact you snuck out on us? Then you followed the enemy into a firefight with no weapon or armor, and we definitely need to discuss the fact you went on the attack and got yourself shot in the process."

"You done?" Vic growled at him. "let's get her fixed up, first."

"Right. Sorry." Ward nodded. "I'm just glad you're okay, little star. I thought we'd lost you back there and it..." he shook his head and moved away. But not before she sensed what he was feeling: a grief so powerful she could feel it even through the drugs and distant pain.

"Wolf? Come back, please."

She waited until Ward was in sight again before she explained. "I felt the same way when I came to on that shuttle, tied up, alone, and scared. I agreed to help Vivian and the Gray's, but that was only because if I said no, they were going to throw me out the airlock." Suddenly she needed them to know that. In case

Vivian said something to make them doubt her intentions.

"Shh. We know you'd never do that," Vic soothed her.

"And I didn't really sneak out. I left a message for you with Tink, and I was going to message you again when I got to my office." All this talking was making her tired again, but she wanted to tell them what had happened.

Ward spoke, his voice tight. "You left us to go back to *work*?"

She closed her eyes, as if shutting down one sense might give her more energy to keep speaking. "Not to work, not exactly. I wanted to let the IAF leadership know about us, so they could decide if they wanted to continue using my services or not."

"You were going to tell them you were dating us?" one of them asked.

"Well, yeah. I mean, humans have rules about therapists falling for their patients. I thought I better tell them before they figured it out on their own."

She didn't need to see their faces to know what they were feeling. Twin surges of affection, joy, and something far more powerful flowed into her and she let it carry her back into the comforting quiet of unconsciousness. She was safe now. She could rest.

He'd been a soldier the first half of his life and an assassin most of the other half, but Vic had never been in a fight like this. The stakes were higher than ever because they had Xori to protect. He glanced down at the sleeping female curled in his arms, her blue coloring so washed out her cheeks and lips were gray.

They'd brought a basic battlefield med-kit with them. It had a few pain-blockers and a selection of wound sealants made to stop someone from bleeding out before they could get to a med-bay. Or, if you were a cyborg, to hold you over until your medi-bots could repair the damage. The problem was, Xori didn't have medi-bots yet. He wouldn't dose her with them unless it was a matter of life and death. She should make that decision for herself, for one thing. But almost as important was the need to keep the military clueless about what Denz was up to. If they found out someone outside their control was producing the nanotech again, it could cause problems for not just Denz, but the whole Haven colony.

They had to keep her safe and get her into the *Malora's* med-bay for treatment. The team's medic was already prepped and waiting to perform the chip extraction and fix her injuries. They just needed to get her there.

"Commander Rossi, we're only a few minutes out. Sit-rep from your end, please," Ward asked.

"Blink and Sabre are in position. Magi was working to take down the ship's systems, but we hit a snag. He swears he got all the auto-defenses, but we can't be sure. Seems like these bastards learned a few things from our last incursions."

He knew Rossi was talking about a pair of raids his

team had done against the Grays. During the first one, they'd freed Nyx. All he knew about the second raid was they'd come back with another freed cyborg, Nyx's clone, Shadow. The rest was classified, and that was fine with him. Nova Force was here for the ship and to gather intelligence. They were here for one reason – to get Xori back, and they'd almost *fraxxed* that up.

A ghost from their past had almost cost them their future. He was still angry with himself for that. Worse, Xori had put herself in harm's way, and by the time they'd realized the danger, it had been too late.

They'd screwed up their reaction, too, slowing each other down and getting in the other's way as they both tried to be the one to take the hit. Xori had known what they'd do, and she'd sacrificed herself to protect them.

He looked down at the beauty in his arms and felt a surge of emotions so strong they nearly brought him to his knees. Ward was right, they didn't deserve her. But that didn't change the fact that she was theirs, and he'd fight to the death to keep her.

"How's she doing?" Ward asked as he checked around yet another corridor intersection. They weren't far from the extraction point, now. They hadn't come across any resistance since they'd killed two females armed with basic blasters, either. Like the men, they'd refused to surrender, so he and Ward had no choice but to kill them.

"Still out of it. Probably for the best. Even with the pain-blockers she's going to hurt every second she's awake."

"Our little hellcat is something else, isn't she?" Ward looked at Xori with a mixture of awe and adoration.

"She is."

"And she didn't leave us."

"Nope." He grinned. "She was planning on making us official."

"She's never going anywhere without one of us again, though," said Ward flatly.

"I'm in full agreement, but I'm pretty sure she's not going to like that idea."

Ward touched her cheek softly. "I don't care. I need her alive, and whole, and safe. She was right, you know. I would have given my life for you and her today." He paused, then added in a quieter voice. "In fact, that's always been the plan."

"I kind of knew that." He'd always suspected, but he hadn't pushed. Hadn't wanted to believe Ward would go down that road. It was something they were going to have to talk about. If they were getting through this, they'd need to stop pretending they were fine and find a way to make it true.

"Did she really say she loved us?" Ward asked a second later.

Vic didn't answer, he just shared the memory with Ward directly, letting him experience it for himself.

It was a good moment, but it didn't last. There was a shimmer in the air in front of them, and Ariel/Vivian appeared again, her face oddly expressionless as she stared them down.

"You can't win."

"Funny, feels like we're winning right now. Nova

Force will find whatever hole you're hiding in, and then they're going to arrest you and use you to tear down the Gray Men." Ward didn't even slow down, he just walked through the projection like it wasn't there at all.

Vic followed his brother's lead, but as he passed through the hologram she laughed. It was a stilted, awkward bleating noise that repeated twice before stopping as suddenly as it started. It sounded oddly artificial.

Vivian continued talking. "You disappoint me. But then, I should be used to that by now. You two had such potential, but you never lived up to it."

He kept walking, resisting the urge to respond. She was trying to distract them again, which meant…*fraxx.* "Run! She's up to something."

He tightened his hold on Xori and sprinted toward their allies. "Rossi, tell everyone to pull back. Go! Go! Go!"

They caught up to the others one corridor later. He flew past, leaving Ward to carry the humans along with him. He heard two surprised shouts, and then they running hell for leather to the ship. He had no idea what was coming, or how long they had, but his instincts were screaming that they were almost out of time.

The commander himself stood watch outside the airlock they'd breached. "Don't stop, run her straight to medical. We're out of here the second you're on board!" Rossi yelled the moment they were in sight.

Rossi's team had made sure they had a map of the basic layout of the *Malora,* so Vic knew exactly where to go. It only took a few seconds to reach the open doors of the med-bay. "Get her settled. I want her secure before we disengage," Caldwell pointed to an empty bed.

Vic placed Xori on it but couldn't bring himself to move away from her side. *"Xori's safe in the med-bay. You good?"* He asked his brother over their personal link.

"I'm good. Take care of her. I'll be there as soon as Rossi stops asking me questions."

"I'm sorry, but you need to let go of her. I can't start the scanner until you're clear." Caldwell pointed to the stretch of wall near the door. "Grab hold of something and hang on tight. Depending on what happens next, this could get bumpy. I'll secure the doctor."

He went where he was told, belatedly noticing that Nyx was already standing there, one hand wrapped around a handle, her feet planted firmly on the deck.

"You're a medic?" he asked as he joined her.

She scoffed. "Hell no. My job is to hurt people. Trip's the one that fixes them afterward. I'm here for him." She jerked her head toward the other bed. Eric Erben was lying on his side, holding a bloody towel to his face. His expression was one of annoyance, not pain, so Vic assumed whatever his injuries were, they weren't critical.

"What happened?" Vic asked.

"That ship's AI is a bitch. It deleted itself before I could lock it down, but it left a surprise for me. Good thing I wasn't fully jacked in or I'd have more than a bloody nose right now."

"You're not supposed to be talking, Magi. Lie down, shut up, and let the system finish scanning you."

Eric rolled his eyes, but he flopped onto his back and didn't say anything else.

"Rank has its uses," Caldwell started to chortle, but then the ship bucked, the engines came to life with a roar, and it was all Vic could do to keep his feet.

"Next verse, same as the first," Eric muttered. "I'm getting really tired of having to evac from the Gray's ships just before they blow them up. Don't they get tired of it?"

"Not so far, anyway," Caldwell said. He was holding fast to a handhold right beside the scanning system for Xori's bed while the fingers of his free hand flew across the screen as he talked.

"Don't let go of that handle. If they blew the ship, the shock wave will catch up with us any second now." Nyx said.

"They do this a lot?"

"Uh huh." Nyx nodded, relaxing slightly as the *Malora* leveled off. "The Grays live by the motto if we can't have it, no one can."

And that was what worried him. Not that he thought the Grays would come for him or Ward again. Vivian had made it clear they were a disappointing experiment, nothing more. But for the others: Nyx, Shadow, and now, Xori? They wouldn't be safe until this fight was over. "We need to kill every last one of these bastards."

"Yes, we do," Nyx agreed, her words edged in ice.

Before Nyx could say anything else, a deep voice boomed out over the ship's comms.

"This is Strak. We are away and clear. Please let go of my ship, now. She doesn't like being groped by anyone but me."

"Huh. No kaboom?" Eric said, then wilted under the medic's gaze and lapsed into silence again.

"And in case you're wondering why we weren't hit with a shock wave, they went with explosive decompression this time. If the wonder twins hadn't told us to haul ass, we'd all be sucking vacuum right now," Strak informed them.

"That sneaky bitch," Vic muttered.

"Who?" Nyx asked.

"Ariel. Or no, she's calling herself Vivian now."

All three of them stared at him for a long moment.

Nyx broke the silence first. "Vivian? Dark hair, hard face, weird laugh?"

"Sounds right. Thing is, that face isn't hers. She stole it from a dead woman, Ariel Coal, our former handler."

"Vivian was on that ship?" Caldwell asked.

He almost said yes, but he couldn't be sure. "All we saw was a hologram. I thought she was there, but now..." he shrugged. The Grays were ruthless and more than capable of killing their own, but she hadn't looked worried while she was trying to distract them, so either she was immune to open vacuum, or she wasn't in any danger.

"She wasn't there in person." Xori joined the conversation. Her voice was soft and her words were mushy as she tried to talk past her split and swollen lips.

"How long have you been awake?" he started toward her, but Caldwell held up a hand.

"Hold on just a few seconds more, scans are almost complete."

Vic stopped, then growled in frustration. "Make it fast."

"I have a cyborg and a Torski as teammates and my commander is named after a dog. Do you really think growling at me is going to work? Dr. Virness, can you confirm what you said before? That Vivian was not on board?"

"I'm pretty sure. The woman I saw on the vid-screen in the shuttle had some odd expressions and movements that I didn't see in her projection. I wondered about that, but it didn't sink in until now. That wasn't a hologram of her, it was a digital avatar. She wasn't being projected in from somewhere else, she was actually there, but as a digital construct. The Grays have all sorts of tech, right? They could do that? Make an avatar of herself so she could…well, sort of be two places at once?"

Vic caught the dark look that passed between the three Nova Force crew. *Fraxx*, the Grays *did* have that kind of tech. Caldwell nodded the all-clear, and Vic went to stand at her side. He rested a hand on her good shoulder and kissed her gently, making sure to avoid the bumps and bruises on her face. "You can tell us more about that later. All I care about right now is how you're doing."

"I'm fine. Well, mostly. But the medic can fix me up, right...?" Xori stared up at Caldwell. "I'm sorry. I have no idea who you are."

The lieutenant gave her a friendly smile and winked at her. "I'm Lieutenant Crispin Charles Caldwell the 15th. But you can call me Trip."

Vic growled again and crowded in closer to Xori. "Are you in pain? Do you want more pain-blockers?" He was pretty sure they were questions the medic should be asking, but he didn't like the idea of the overly charming lieutenant saying *anything* to his female.

"Pain's there, but it's not going to kill me." She touched her lip and frowned. "I remember getting shot, but why does my face hurt?"

"Because you took a round to the shoulder and landed face-first on the deck."

"You have a split lip, a chipped tooth, a broken nose, some contusions, and I see they implanted you with one of their chips. I've got a field up to block any signals and we'll have that out of you soon." Caldwell looked over at Vic. "Nice job with the dressing on her shoulder. Nothing here we can't fix."

"I'm sorry, blossom."

She frowned at him. "For what?"

"You got hurt because I wasn't there."

She huffed. "Don't do that. This isn't your fault. None of it is. I got kidnapped because the Grays are power-hungry *gurani*. I got shot because I choose to make myself a target."

"But I should have—"

She raised her one good hand to stop him talking. "You should have what? Taken all my choices away from me? Forced me to comply with how you wanted things to go? Because that's what the Grays do, and you're not like them. You're one of the good guys." Her hand fell back to her side like she was too tired to hold it up anymore.

"Okay. I think that's enough talking. I need to put you under so I can fix your shoulder and get that chip out of your neck. You ready, Dr. Virness?" Caldwell asked.

"One more question first, please. Where's Wolf? Is he alright?"

"We're both fine. He's debriefing the others. He'll be here soon."

"Good." Her eyes fluttered closed. "Alright. I'm ready."

"See you soon, blossom."

The medic moved to her side, injecting her with something that made her relax with a soft sigh that nearly tore his heart out of his chest.

"She's our everything," he told Caldwell as he reclaimed his spot by the wall.

The blond man nodded. "I'll have her patched up and resting comfortably before we make it back to Astek. A day or so in the med-center there, and then you can take her home. Now, I need you both to step outside, please. And Nyx, you can take Eric with you, but he needs rest, okay?"

"Yes sir. Come on, Magi. Lets get your sexy, slightly singed ass back to our quarters."

Vic followed them out into the corridor, then connected to Ward. *"She's going into surgery now. Their medic says she's going to be fine."*

"I hate not being with her.

"Yeah, me too." What Xori had said about choices kept bouncing around his brain. He'd have to tell Ward about that, because she was right. They were going to have to respect her decisions, even when they didn't agree with them.

That realization was followed by another one. One that made everything stand still as, between one breath and the next, reality and his perception of it... of himself... was rewritten. He wasn't responsible for anyone else's choices. Not Xori's, or Ward's, or anyone's. The team he'd once led weren't his team anymore, they were his family.

Somewhere deep inside him, a knot loosened a little, and he walked like the gravity was a little less than it had been. It was yet another gift Xori had given him. He smiled as he made his way through the ship to Ward. They had a lot to talk about, and even more planning to do.

CHAPTER FOURTEEN

WARD LEANED against the wall outside the med-center and watched for potential threats. Not that he really expected the Gray's to make a move this soon, but he wasn't risking Xori's safety. Apparently, that sentiment was shared by the members of his family, because Toro stood on the other side of the corridor, watching over *him*.

It had been like that since they'd left the *Malora*—everyone taking shifts, watching out for each other, ensuring no one was alone. He had the feeling it was going to be like this for the foreseeable future. The data stick Xori had brought with her was full of information their enemy should never have been able to gain access to. They'd been more vulnerable than any of them had realized.

People were scrambling to make sure it never happened again. The only place that hadn't been compromised was the Nova Club. Apparently, not even the Gray Men could find a way through the layers of security Phaedra Kari had installed before she'd left. It was the safest place on the station, bar none, which was a good thing, because damned near everyone he cared about lived there. He glanced back at the door to the med-center. Everyone but Xori...but if things went well today, that was going to change.

He started whistling as he stood watch, counting down the minutes until he could see Xori again. Alyson had made it clear that she wanted her patient left alone to rest and heal. Not even Archer had been allowed to see Xori, which made Ward feel a little better about being tossed out by the feisty blonde doctor.

She didn't seem to mind them taking turns standing guard, though. In fact, she found it amusing. "All things come full circle," she'd said by way of explanation.

That jogged his memory. Dirk, Blade, and Lance had once stood watch outside the med-center, almost exactly in the same spot he was now, only they were guarding Alyson against a different threat that time – him.

Full circle, indeed.

He reached out to his brother through their link. Not because he needed an update, but because it would help pass the time. *"How's it going?"*

"The same as it was ten minutes ago when you last asked me that question. You need a new hobby."

"But annoying you is my favorite pastime. You know that."

"If you keep distracting me, we won't get this done in time."

"Maybe that's my devious plan to keep you away so I can steal a few more minutes with our girl."

"You can't steal what's freely given. Just let me know when you want me to join the two of you."

They were identical in more ways than not, so it wasn't a surprise they'd fallen for the same female. Sharing her affection, though, was going to take more communication than either of them had realized. Especially because until recently, Ward hadn't planned to be sharing her for long. He'd believed that all he could hope for was a few glimmers of light from the brightest star in his sky. *Her.* *"I just need to talk with her first."*

"I know." And Vic did know, because they'd finally opened about the darkness they'd both been carrying since they'd become the Reaper. They'd talked a lot during the time they'd on the Malora, and the conversations had continued since they're returned to the Drift the previous day. Sometimes they'd spoken in person, other times across their link.

Xori had made that conversation possible. Not just because they'd faced old demons while rescuing her, but because she'd known that both of them would try to sacrifice themselves to save the others. She knew them better than anyone. Better than they knew themselves. That revelation had rocked them both and led to some long overdue confessions. They'd been hiding their guilt from each other, both of them convinced they owed the other one a debt they couldn't repay.

He shook his head. They'd been idiots, and she

loved them, anyway. She knew them so well. Too well. Which is why he was certain she already knew what he needed to tell her, but he still needed to say the words. Then he could to tell her why he'd changed his mind. He wasn't going anywhere. Not if she wanted him to stay.

Five minutes later, the doors opened, and Alyson smiled at him. "She's ready."

"More than ready." Xori's voice added, though she was still out of sight. "I've been cooped up in strange rooms for days, and most of that time I wasn't even wearing my own clothes."

Ward stepped into the doorway, grinning. "Whatever you need, little star. Just ask and I'll make it happen."

Xori cried out in delight and ran to him, throwing her good arm around his waist and hugging him tight.

He cradled her against him, bowing his head to nuzzle the crown of her hair. It was the first time he'd been able to do more than hold her hand since she'd been injured, and having her back in his arms, alive and well, healed parts of him he hadn't known were hurting. "I missed you too," he murmured.

"I want to go home, now."

"That's why I'm here." He looked up at Alyson. "What do I need to know before I take her out of here?"

"She needs rest, good food, and time to heal. Don't let her lift anything heavier than a glass of water for a few days, and if it hurts, Xori, take a pain-blocker."

Xori nodded without moving her head from his chest. "I will."

"We'll take care of her. Starting with a ride to her quarters."

Xori raised her head to stare at him. "It's not even a ten-minute walk."

"So it will be a very short ride. It's one of the new hover-carts they're bringing in for the guests at the gala."

"Oh! I haven't even seen one of those, yet. How did you…" She trailed off with a laugh. "Tianna?"

"She insisted."

"I bet she did." Xori kept one arm around him as she turned to smile at Alyson. "Thank you for making me rest, even if I didn't want to."

"You're very welcome." Alyson crossed the empty waiting room to give them both a hug.

Ward hugged her back, and another dark corner of his soul filled with light. He'd apologized to Alyson more than once, but this was something more than her forgiveness. It was a gift he'd always be grateful for. "Thank you."

He carried Xori to the cart that had arrived while he was inside, setting her down in her seat as carefully as he could.

"I won't break, you know," she laughed.

"Indulge me." He'd seen her broken, and the image of her lying bloodied and still on the hangar floor would haunt him for the rest of his life. He never wanted to see her hurt again. But for that to happen, she had to say yes.

The cart was self-driving, so he took a seat beside her, made sure she was settled, and gave the cart verbal directions to her quarters. They set off, but he could sense her unease and the way she kept scanning the crowd.

"If you're worried about Tesk or his entourage, don't be. While we were off-station, Corp-Sec caught some of them harassing the Pheran vendors. The offenders are already on their way back to Phera Prime."

"They didn't hurt anyone, did they?"

"No one hurt, nothing damaged. Tesk and the remaining Pheran visitors had their access to this station restricted to certain areas to make sure it doesn't happen again."

Her shoulders sagged a little as she laughed, sounding relieved. "Tianna again?"

"And Corp-Sec. None of them are allowed to come back to Astek again. Corp-Sec issued them all lifetime bans."

She smiled. "Good."

After that, she stopped looking for danger and seemed to enjoy the trip. It was a smooth ride, and in only a few minutes they were at the security check point that marked the border between the regular station and the military base housed within it.

Xori looked around the newly fortified location with surprise. There were double the guards and clearly-marked corridors for traffic moving in and out of the area. As well, barriers had been installed near to each pair of guards, the transparent walls forming a protective shield.

They stepped out of the cart while their identities

were scanned and biometrically verified before they were waved through. It was all done quickly and efficiently, and he could tell Xori hated every second of it.

The cart wasn't allowed beyond the checkpoint, so they started walking the last of the distance on foot.

"This is because of what happened to me? I did this?"

He took her hand. "No. The Gray's did this when they hacked the security footage from this post and tried to make it look like you'd returned home. All these changes are what happens when a big, bad military force finds out they've been compromised."

"I'm going to have to go through that whole process every time I want to leave or come back." She didn't sound pleased.

"Maybe. That's one of the things we need to talk about. But first, let's get you home."

She had to lead him to her quarters. He had no idea where they were, though the feel of the place was familiar. He'd spent enough of his life on bases and warships to recognize the look. Nondescript corridors that smelled vaguely of cleanser. Clean but well-worn floors. Posted signs with so many abbreviations it barely resembled Galactic Standard.

Her door was identical to every other one they'd passed—the only thing marking it as hers was the name displayed beside it.

He knew her place was safe, but it was still difficult for him to hold back and let her enter first.

"I see I had visitors." He came in behind her and

found her grinning up at a large holographic banner that read "Welcome home, feel better soon."

There were fresh flowers on a small table, and someone had loosed a swarm of party orbs inside. They swirled and danced a few inches below the ceiling, lighting up the room with a constantly changing light show.

"They wanted to make your homecoming special, but Alyson vetoed any kind of celebration until you were fully recovered."

She bent down to smell the bouquet of orange, crimson and yellow blooms. He had no idea what kind they were, but she seemed to like them. He'd have to find out where the women had found them, so they could buy her more. "Very sneaky. They must have done this while they were getting me something to wear."

"Very sneaky," he agreed. He'd been busy working on her office while this part of the plan had been accomplished.

Now the moment had come, he wasn't sure how to begin, and he found himself stalling. "Do you need anything? A drink? Something to eat?"

She smiled at him. "I need you and a hot shower. Preferably at the same time."

All his plans to talk to her went out the airlock and he had her back in his arms in less than a second. "Whatever you want."

She tipped her head up to meet his kiss, and he let himself get lost in the details of her body. She was warm and soft, her lips still slightly swollen where they hadn't completely healed yet. He claimed her mouth gently, tasting the subtle sweetness of her kiss and letting the delicate scent of her body wrap itself around his senses.

"I love you," The words came out of their own accord. He hadn't planned on saying it yet. He'd wanted to take care of her, first, but he couldn't wait any longer to tell her what she meant to him. He'd hidden it from himself too long as it was. He didn't want to keep it from her another second.

"I love you too." Her fingers stroked his cheek, then slid back to tangle in his hair as she pulled him in for another kiss, this one hungrier and harder than he expected.

"You're still bruised," he reminded her.

"But I'm also still here. We are all still here, and I need to celebrate that."

"Do you want me to tell Vic to join us?"

She shook her head. "Not yet. Right now, I just want you."

"And later?"

She blushed, her skin darkening until her stripes were almost black. "Later, I'm going to be greedy and want you both."

"There's nothing greedy about wanting to be with the men you love." He hadn't meant to talk about this until Vic got here, but he wouldn't pretend it wasn't what they wanted. "We want this. You. Everything."

Her smile was brighter than any star in the cosmos. "Yes."

He crushed her to him and kissed her again. Not

gently this time, but with all the need and fire coursing through him. She rose on her toes, her talons stroking across the back of his skull with just enough force to sting a little. He drank her down like the sweetest wine, lifted her into his arms, and carried her to what he hoped was the sanitation room. If it was the bedroom, then she wasn't going to get her shower for a while.

"Good guess," she murmured.

The room was basic and utilitarian, just like the rest of her quarters, but it wasn't cramped and the shower was more than big enough for the two of them. He turned on the water and kept testing it as he stripped Xori out of her clothes. By time he was done, the water was the perfect temperature and steam was starting to fill the space.

He let her go in first, then shucked off his clothes and dropped them in a heap beside hers. If this went the way he hoped, he wouldn't need them again for a day or more. The last time he'd had Xori naked and in his arms, he'd thought it was his only chance to be with her and he'd been trying to keep enough distance to make it easier for him to walk away. This time would be different. He wasn't going anywhere, and if she agreed to what they planned on offering her, neither would Xori.

She hadn't known how much she missed her males until she'd seen Ward at the door of the med-center. Every lingering ache and pain had vanished, and once she had her arms around him, she felt like she could breathe again.

She'd only slept because she'd been sedated, but even then, it hadn't been a good sleep. What rest she'd gotten had been restless and haunted by nightmares where she watched her lovers die over and over again. She didn't expect those dreams to go away any time soon. Or the sense of unease that struck the moment they'd stepped out into the chaos and noise of the station. Even knowing it was likely, she'd been surprised at how anxious she'd felt. She'd only managed as well as she had because Ward's presence had grounded her. She'd leaned into his strength to bolster her own, and she'd likely need to for a little while longer, at least. She was getting a crash course in so many of the experiences and challenges her patients faced, and it gave her new insights into how to help them.

Ward joined her in the shower as the hot water poured over her in a blissful cascade of heat, washing away any lingering traces of the pain and fear she'd experienced in the last few days.

When she reached for the cleanser, he caught her hand by the wrist and drew it gently back to her side. "Let me do this. You just relax and enjoy."

She shivered at the rough note of desire in his voice and leaned against his chest, eyes closed, basking in both the heat and his attention.

He undid her hair from its braid, drawing the wet strands over her shoulder as he smoothed a handful of cleansing gel over her back. He moved slowly, his touch somewhere between a caress and a light massage that felt wonderful.

"You ever think about switching careers? Instead of working the gaming tables, you could charge a fortune as a masseuse."

His laughter rumbled by her ear and sent a delightful shiver down her spine. "I don't see that happening. The only body I want to touch is yours."

"Hmm. Good point."

His teeth closed on her earlobe as his hands swept lower, working out the aches in her lower back. "I like this."

"Me too. Best back rub, ever."

"Not that. It's being alone with you. Apart from a few one-on-one sessions, it's never been just the two of us."

"You're right." She tipped her head back until she could see his face. "I guess that means we need more than one date night. You and me, me and Vic, and all three of us together. I'm going to have a very full social calendar."

"Date nights sounds good." He poured more cleanser into his hand and started to work it through her hair. She groaned in pleasure as he massaged her scalp, the sensation equally relaxing and arousing.

"Damn it, I had so many good intentions, but if you keep making those sounds...."

She groaned again, louder this time, and the next second he'd spun her around to face him.

"Last warning." His voice was as deep as a rockslide now, all rumble and growl. She loved him like this, because she knew that as dangerous as he was, he'd never hurt her.

She reached between them and wrapped her fingers around the hard shaft of his cock. She'd felt it pressed against her back as he'd washed her and knew he was as aroused as she was.

His head fell back, his cock jerking in her hand as he groaned her name. The water flowed over him, and for a moment she was reminded of the fountains that decorated so many of the public squares back home, filled with sculptured bodies of stone cavorting through the streams of water forever. Eternal, just like Vic and Ward were, or near enough as to make no difference. As far as anyone knew, cyborgs didn't age. Decades from now, they could still be together, but it wouldn't be the same. *She* wouldn't be the same,

She pushed the thought aside. That was a problem for another day. Maybe one that would solve itself in time. It didn't change the fact that these were the two she wanted to spend her life with, however long that might be.

Ward's hands cupped her cheeks. "Tell me what you need."

"You."

His hips jerked, moving her cock against her fingers. "You already have that."

"Inside me."

His lips curved up in a smile that made her heart stutter. "That, I can do."

She expected him to pick her up and take her against the wall or carry her off to bed. Instead, he bent down to kiss her. It was a slow, molten kiss. One that made her knees quiver and her toes curl. He took his time, nibbling and tasting, sucking her lower lip into his mouth, his hands still cradling her face.

He moved slowly and deliberately down her body, tracing his way from her mouth to her jaw to her throat. The touch of his lips blended with the flow of water over her skin and soon every part of her sang with need.

She buried her hands in the dark length of his hair in an attempt to hurry him, but it was like trying to bend steel.

He laughed, catching her arms at the wrists and drawing them together, holding her captive with one hand as he dropped the other to one of her breasts and tweaking the nipple. "No rushing. You're supposed to be relaxing, remember?"

She tugged at her wrists and huffed at him, the sound coming out more like a wet splutter in the stream of hot water. "Difficult, stubborn, male."

He leaned down, drawing his tongue across one sensitive nipple. "You forgot a word."

She shivered and bit her lip to muffle the gasp that rose as he touched her so expertly. "Mmh?"

"Yours." He ran his thumb across the pebbled nub of her other breast. "I am *your* difficult, stubborn male."

"That you are. Both of you." She nuzzled the top of his head. She already thought of them as her *vardo,* her mates. She wasn't sure when it had happened, just like she didn't know when her feelings for them had solidified, moving from affection and desire to something far more powerful.

He drew her nipple into the heat of his mouth and she arched into him, need rushing to the forefront of her awareness. His hand slid down her stomach to her pussy, and when his fingers pressed inside her folds, she moved her feet farther apart and bucked against his hand.

He circled her clit with his fingertip, mirroring the move with his tongue around the peak of her breast until it was almost too much, and yet still not enough.

"More." The single word fell from her lips, half demand, half plea.

He hummed in approval and released her wrists then stepped back and lowered himself to his knees. "Back against the wall. I don't want you to slip and hurt yourself."

She reached behind her, found the tiled surface, and backed up until the cool ceramic pressed against her skin. He prowled over to her on his hands and knees, like a hunter approaching his prey *Veth*, she liked him this way, dominant, confident. She could feel what he needed, and she gave it to him because it was what she wanted, too. "I am yours."

He smiled up at her, guiding her leg over his shoulder as he knelt at her feet. It was a supplicant's pose, but he wasn't the one submitting. "Mine."

She barely had time to register the way his tone made the word into a declaration before he was between her thighs, his mouth on her sex and his fingers sliding into her channel.

She slapped her palms against the wall, bracing herself against the shocking suddenness of his actions. He wasn't teasing her anymore. He pumped his hand hard and fast while his tongue lashed across her clit with merciless intensity.

All she could do was take what he was giving her, riding each wave of pleasure as it came. A low rhythmic rumbling rose from her throat.

He added another finger and curved them inward, so that every stroke hit nerve endings that increased her pleasure. It was more than she could take, and she came hard, only staying on her feet because he reached up to steady her, his hands on her hips as she rocked and shuddered through her orgasm.

When he moved away, he was grinning and throwing off so much smug satisfaction she could feel it without even trying. "You *kyrned*."

"You know what that is?" The low, throaty purring noise her species made in the thrall of ecstasy wasn't something many outside her race knew about.

"Hell yes. I studied." He winked at her. "We both did."

She blushed. "So did I."

He gathered her into his arms, kissed her softly, and turned off the water. "I want to hear all about what you learned, with demonstrations, of course. But first, I think we should get dried off and into bed. There's something I need you to do for me."

She nodded. She didn't know what he wanted, but if it was within her power to do it, she would.

CHAPTER FIFTEEN

THERE WAS something deeply satisfying about taking care of Xori. Ward had enjoyed pampering her, washing her hair and soothing some of her aches away. The way she'd leaned into him with complete trust and acceptance warmed his heart and made him love her even more.

After they'd dried each other off, she'd led him to her bedroom. Like the rest of her quarters, it was basic and bland, but she'd added a few of her own touches. A handful of holo-pics set out on a dresser, a cream-colored rug on the floor, and the screen on one wall was set to look like a small window that looked out over the rooftops of some unknown world with a lapis-blue sky.

"Phera Prime?"

Xori curled up against the pillows and patted a space beside her with a playful smile. "Yes. My mother took that picture and sent it to me."

"Do you miss them?"

"Very much. I'd like to go back to see them one day, but they won't hear of it. Too risky."

"Like what happened the night you stopped me from killing Tesk? That's one of the reasons the Grays abducted you, isn't it?"

She sighed. "It was. They've been watching me for months. When they saw the footage of that night, they were smart enough to guess what it meant."

"I'm sorry." He'd seen the files they'd stolen from her office, and the projects they planned on making her work on. Her training and knowledge combined with her abilities had made her a target too tempting to resist, and it was his fault they'd learned her secret.

"You were protecting me. I chose to protect you. I don't regret what I did that night. But…it's safer for me if I don't go home again. If I did it again somewhere with more Pherans who understood what it might mean…" She shook her head. "I can't risk it. It's not just about me." She gave him a small smile. "It runs through maternal lines. If I were caught, they'd take my mother, too. Even though her abilities are far less powerful than mine."

That stunned him to silence for a second. "But she's mated. Settled. Happy."

"It wouldn't matter."

"Someday, I'd really like it if we discovered a race that wasn't *fraxxed* up in some way."

"I'd like that, too."

A thought occurred to him. "Maybe we can bring them here? We know people with ships. It's not like they'd have to pay for anything. It could be a vacation for them."

Her face lit up with a hopeful smile he'd slay a thousand men to see again. "Do you think we could?"

He laughed. "Sweetheart, you're friends with Zura Watson and Tianna *fraxxing* Astor. If you told them you wanted to see your parents, I suspect they'd move the stars themselves to make it happen. Vic and I would help, too."

She squealed in delight and hugged him, and he knew that somehow, they'd see it done. Family was important, and he'd like to meet the beings who had raised the female he fallen in love with.

Love. Even now he'd said the words, it was still a surprise to him. After he'd been freed, he wasn't sure he would ever be capable of feeling that kind of emotion for anyone, not even his family. But he was. Xori had helped him with that. She'd believed in him even when he'd been certain he had no future at all, never mind one that included her. She'd given it all back to him. First she'd helped him reconnect with his family, then with friends who had become family. And now there was Xori, the female he wanted to create a family with.

Her hug turned into a kiss that dragged him out of his thoughts and into a reality where he was naked and tangled up with the most beautiful female in creation. He rolled them over so she was pinned beneath him, making the bed creak in protest.

"What kind of paperwork do you think I'll have to fill out if we break this bed tonight?"

"Let's try not to find out. Archer's still grumpier

than a Nantari rhino with a toothache over the fact we didn't wait for Rossi and his team like we promised."

She laughed and raised her head to kiss him lightly. "He'll get over it. He's spent enough time around the Nova Club cyborgs to know that was never going to happen. None of you would ever stand by and wait while someone you cared for was in trouble."

"Never," he agreed. "And apparently, neither would you. When I saw you charging the guy about to shoot us…"

"I was protecting the beings *I* care about." She touched his cheek softly. "Because I knew that if I didn't do something, I'd lose you."

"Vic told me you'd said that. I didn't realize you knew."

"Despite everything I did to help you, you were still convinced you weren't worthy. Not of a good life, or happiness, or love. You kept finding ways to punish yourself. It hurt my heart to see you do that to yourself, and I was frustrated I couldn't seem to reach you."

He turned to kiss her fingers. "I think we can safely say your message got through. I'm done with all that."

She smiled at him, her eyes softening. "I hope so. But if you're not, if you ever feel doubts, I can help you see all the ways you're worthy."

"That's what I wanted to ask you. I want you to do that thing again."

She frowned slightly. "You want me to take away the darkness again? Are you sure?"

It was his turn to smile. "No, love. There's no need

to take it away. I want you to see for yourself that it isn't there anymore."

Her frown vanished, and she lay her hand gently on his cheek. "I have your permission?"

"Always."

He felt her connect with him. It was subtle, but he sensed her energy around him, and he realized it was familiar. It was the same feeling he'd had on the *Enigma*, when he'd known she was there even before he'd seen her dash through the doors, and before that, when they'd been pacing the deck of the *Faerie Queene*. Later, he'd have to ask her about that. How had they been able to sense her when she was the empathic one?

She uttered a soft sigh. "It's gone. How?"

"You're, my shining star, Xori Virness. You drove away the darkness with your light."

There were tears shimmering in her silver eyes as she stared up at him. "That is the most beautiful thing anyone has ever said to me."

He grinned and leaned in to kiss her, but stopped a hairsbreadth from her lips to whisper. "I'm sending a copy of this conversation to Vic right now. Got anything you'd like to add, apart from the fact that I'm clearly your favorite?"

She laughed and nodded. "Fox, wherever you are, whatever you're doing, I want you to drop it and get over here. I miss you."

Ward copied the memory and sent it to his brother without further comment.

"Five minutes," Vic responded only a few seconds

later. *"And when the hell did you learn to be that charming?"*

"I was made like this. Pure perfection. They must have forgotten to upload that part of your program."

"Vic is on his way. If you need anything, food, a drink, or a pain-blocker, now's your chance, because once we let him in, we've got plans for you."

"Once Vic gets here, I'll have everything I need."

Having Ward here, in her bed, made it feel real. Their first time together had been a lavish fantasy. The fancy ship, the food, the decadent luxury of their private suite. When she'd left the *Faerie Queene*, she'd felt a little like a character in a children's tale, the poor, lower caste female sneaking back to her old life after one enchanted night pretending to be someone else. Not anymore.

When Ward rose to let Victor in, she stayed where she was, surrounded by familiar things, and waited for her males to return. The thought made her smile. Her males. Her parents were going to need a little time to come to terms with that, but if they could meet Vic and Ward, they'd understand how happy she was. Or how happy she could be if this worked out. There were still so many things they needed to talk about, including the fact she would age, and they wouldn't. They definitely had to talk about that. *But maybe not tonight.*

Ward walked back in, naked and grinning.

"You didn't get dressed first? What if someone else had been at the door?" she asked.

Ward folded his arms across his chest. "You expecting anyone else?"

"Well, no," she admitted. "But someone could have been walking by. That's a public corridor."

"And if they had, they'd have learned that you are no longer a single female and your boyfriends are big enough to keep you protected and *very* well satisfied."

"So much for charming," Vic muttered, elbowing his brother aside so he could get to her.

He perched on the edge of her bed but didn't reach for her. "Hey, blossom. How you feeling?"

"Wonderful. Ward took good care of me. But I'd feel even better if you'd stop hovering and kiss me hello. I won't break."

A shadow darkened his amber eyes for a second. "I will never forget seeing you on the ground, all banged up and bleeding. I don't ever…" He stopped and shook his head.

"I know. Honestly, I'm hoping to avoid getting shot again. I really can't recommend anything about the experience."

He smiled and leaned in to brush a tender kiss to her lips. "I'll make you a deal. I'll try to avoid it if you do."

"Agreed," she said.

The mattress dipped as Ward climbed back into bed and did his best to stretch out without taking up too much space, then coaxed her to snuggle in beside him. "Don't want you to get cold while you're waiting for Vic to stop talking and join us."

Vic rolled his eyes. "An asteroid on a collision

course has more subtlety than you do, but point taken." He rose and stripped off his clothes, which she idly noticed were streaked with what looked like paint and metal shavings.

"Put those down the laundry chute if you want to. What were you doing to get them so dirty?"

"Mine are in the bathroom. Want to pop those in to get cleaned, too?" Ward smirked and pointed across the hall. "Since I'm busy keeping Xori warm, and all."

Vic stalked out, gathered up both their clothes and dropped them into the laundry chute outside the bedroom door. When he came back in, she took a moment to enjoy the view. Golden skin, dark hair, and hands that could deal out damage or comfort with equal skill. He had the predatory grace of a hunter, a body built for war, and a heart filled with courage and compassion. She reached for him, and he was at her side in a second, claiming her mouth with a slow, heated kiss as he settled in beside her.

She turned, so she was on her back, and both males propped their heads up on their hands so they were looking down at her. "This is what I needed. Both of you here with me."

"Us too," Ward murmured, taking one of her hands.

"So much." Vic took her other hand. For a moment, they were both silent, but she sensed they wanted to say something else, so she waited.

"In fact, we'd like it if we could be together like this every night," Ward said at last.

"Here?" she asked, hoping she sounded calmer than she felt. This was what she wanted. *They* were what she wanted. Her species bonded for life, and once they recognized they had found their lifemates, things usually moved fast. Humans were different, though. Sometimes they moved quickly, other than it could be years before relationships became permanent. She hadn't been sure what her lovers would want, and there'd been no time to talk about it.

Vic squeezed her hand. "If that's what you want, but we had something else in mind."

"Something safer," Ward added.

"Safer than here?" She couldn't imagine anywhere being more secure. Especially with the added measures she'd seen coming in today.

"Your abduction led to a station-wide security audit. Turns out, most of the station has been compromised to one degree or another," Ward said.

"Only one place hadn't been touched. The Nova Club. It seems her protocols are so good not even the Gray's can get past them. It's the safest place in the station, and it's our home," Vic paused, and his next words came out in a deep rumble. "We want it to be your home, too."

She gripped both their hands tight. "Yes. I'd like that."

Both men exhaled at the same moment, their relief strong enough she could feel it wash over her like it was a physical thing.

"You didn't know if I'd say yes?" she asked.

"Well, uh. We hoped…" Ward said,

"But, no. We weren't sure." Vic finished.

She wondered if they had even noticed they were

finishing each other sentences. They were more in synch with each other than she'd ever seen them. She sat up, still keeping hold of their hands. "I believe you are my *vardo*. My mates. The males I love and want to spend my life with. Even if that life will be far shorter than yours. I'll grow old and die long before you will." And there it was, the fear she hadn't spoken aloud until now. If they were doing this, they needed to be honest about everything.

Vic reached over and picked up something from her bedside table. "No, blossom, you won't, not if you don't want to."

He held up a compression injector. "This was part of what we wanted to talk to you about."

She frowned. "What's that?"

"A present from Denz. He's been working with the Vardarians to improve the nanotech Zale created."

A rush of emotions hit her so hard she couldn't catch her breath. She gasped and fell back against the bed. When she could finally speak, she managed to squeak two words past her lips in a squeaky voice. "Medi-bots?"

"For you. You'd heal faster, have better endurance, a higher metabolism," Vic started.

"And you'd live as long as we will, assuming none of us gets shot again," Ward said.

She looked at the injector, then at the two of them. A lifetime together.

"Be our *vardi*," Ward murmured, using the Pheran word for female mate.

"Say yes," Vic added.

It was the easiest decision she'd ever had to make. With them, she'd never have to choose between security and freedom. They knew her secrets, and she knew theirs. They could be happy together. They *would* be happy together. "Yes."

They both grinned at her and then smacked their palms together. "She said yes!" Ward whooped. "Quick. Make this permanent before she comes to her senses."

"I'm never changing my mind," she informed them. "You're mine."

"Damn right you are. Ready?" Vic asked.

"Very." She'd never been surer of anything. She turned her head, exposing her throat. It was the opposite side to where Beta had inserted the chip, and the symmetry felt right. One had injection had been to enslave her, this one would set her free.

There was a hiss, a brief sting, and it was done.

She waited a second, not sure what to expect, but nothing happened. "I don't feel any different."

"It will take time for the medi-bots to start replicating, but in an hour or so there won't be any traces of your injuries left. You're as safe as we can make you." Vic winked at her.

She decided to make another confession. "Good, because I'm not comfortable going out in public right now. It's going to take me a while to get over that."

"We'll help." Vic said. "And we made some changes to your office while you were recuperating. You'll be safe there, too."

"What? When? Have you two slept at all?"

"No," they both answered at once. "One of us stood

watch outside the med-center while the other worked on stuff. We took turns. The Grays won't be able to access your files again. They're locked down in ways I don't understand, but Phaedra herself promised it's secure. There's a stronger door, a panic alarm, and a bunch of other changes."

"So that's why there was paint on your shirt?"

Vic smiled. "Yeah. Minor repairs after we were finished the construction phase."

"I don't deserve the two of you. Thank you." She still needed to tell her other patients about the breach, but at least now she could promise it wouldn't happen again. Her *vardo* had been awake all night, taking care of her needs while she healed. She was so blessed to have them in her life.

There were tears in her eyes as she rose up to kiss them, first Ward, then Victor. That kiss led to another, then another, and soon her joy was joined by a passion that burned like rocket fuel through her veins.

"Do you trust us?" Ward asked, his words caressing her ear.

"Always."

"Any pain?" Vic asked.

She thought about that for a moment and shook her head. "None."

"Then roll onto your side with your back to Ward. We're going to take care of you, blossom. All you have to do is relax and let us love you."

She did as he said, rolling onto her side and letting them guide her with gentle hands.

Ward drew her topmost leg up and back, draping it

over his muscular thigh. She could feel his cock pressing against her ass, and it dawned on her what they wanted to do. Arousal made her pussy slick and her blood hum. "Together?"

Vic gave her a hot-eyed look that made her shiver in anticipation of what was to come. "Together."

She nodded, and he reached over to the bedside table again. She'd been so busy enjoying the view when he'd walked back in naked, she'd completely missed what had been in his hands. He showed her the packet of barrier gel he held. It would make what they planned far easier for everyone and let her experience having both of them inside her at once.

Ward reached around to toy with her breast, nibbling gently on her ear. He kept hitting sensitive spots that made her gasp and shiver, her arousal ratcheting up with every touch. Vic opened the packet and spread the gel over his hands, and then handed it to Ward, who did the same. They coordinated their movements, stroking both her entrances at the same time, working the gel carefully into every nook and crevice.

Vic leaned in to kiss her as he worked his fingers across her clit, while Ward slipped a finger into her back channel. It was an intense feeling, somewhere between pleasure and pain, but it faded quickly and she relaxed again.

"That's right, blossom, just relax. You tell us if it gets to be too much." Vic's voice was thick with desire and his amber eyes were bright as he kissed her without closing his eyes. "You are so fraxxing beautiful."

They took their time, preparing her body slowly and with a breathtaking level of focus and skill. They brought her to the brink of orgasm and held her there, stroking and teasing, both of them taking turns kissing and touching her until she was lost in sensations she'd never experienced before. When she came the first time, they barely gave her a moment to recover before they started building her up all over again. Ward added another finger, stretching her until she knew she was ready for the next step.

"Need you both," she whispered.

"We'll be gentle," Ward promised before pulling free of her body and replacing his fingers with the thick head of his cock. He pressed into her in one slow, steady motion, her body giving way to his with just enough resistance to make her flesh burn without ever crossing over into true pain.

"Breathe, little one. I've got you," Ward's voice was tight, but he held still, keeping them locked together until she could relax again.

He nibbled on her ear lobe to distract her while Vic kept rubbing her clit, and it it didn't take long for the discomfort to be drowned out by the pleasure again. Ward eased himself deeper into her body, and by the time he was fully seated inside her, Vic had shifted his position so his cock was at the entrance to her pussy and his gaze was locked on hers.

"I love you," he told her as he carefully slid his cock a few inches inside her, filling her impossibly full.

"We both love you," Ward said.

She wanted to say she loved them, too, but when

she opened her mouth, all that came out was a soft purring noise as she *kyrnned*, her arousal heightened to the point she couldn't speak.

"That is the sexiest sound I have ever heard," Vic said.

"Agreed." Ward touched her hip. "You ready for more, sweetheart?"

She nodded and *kyrnned* louder. She didn't want more, she wanted *everything*. The smallest of movements any of them made filled her with unimaginable levels of pleasure. She couldn't wait to fall into whatever blissful madness would come when they claimed her fully.

Ward moved first, his hand on her hip to steady her as he withdrew and Vic surged into her body. Back and forth, the two of them sharing her, making her the focus of all their desires. It was intoxicating, and there was nothing she could do but surrender to them both.

She was so far gone in her pleasure she forgot to restrain her gift. She became aware of their emotions, the needs and wants of the body as well as the love and light in their hearts. She took it all in until everything was a blur of joy and bliss that filled her completely.

She came hard, her cries captured by Victor's mouth as she shuddered to climax between them. Her body tightened around both of them and they groaned. Their motions sped up, and before she had finished riding out the aftershocks of her release, her lovers were coming, too.

A subtle, spicy scent filled the air, and a sense of deep satisfaction rolled through her as she recognized what she'd done. They were marked with her scent now, and every Pheran on the station would know they were hers.

Ward nuzzled her ear, his breath still coming in hard pants. "You marked us."

"I did."

"And you...." Vic met her gaze, his cock still throbbing inside her. "I felt you. You linked to us somehow."

"Wait, you could feel that?"

Both men grunted in the affirmative. That... shouldn't have been possible. There were a few stories about powerfully gifted *m'bari* bonding to their mates, but that's all they were, stories. Her *vardo* weren't even the same species. But...they were her mates. Now and forever. She reached for them both, taking hold of their hands and sharing her joy with them, not sure how to do it, but wanting them to know how happy she was, and how much she loved them. Her family. Her mates. Her everything.

Their feelings flowing back to her, wrapping her in emotions so powerful there were no words to describe them. There were tears in her eyes as she held fast to them both, enjoying this moment and reveling in the knowledge that they had all made their choice, and they had chosen each other. "I love you both."

"And we love you. Always," Vic whispered.

"And forever," Ward added.

EPILOGUE

Xori sat in the VIP section of the Nova Club, content to listen to the other females as they chatted. It was only mid-morning, but the place was already busy as a steady flow of customers came to eat, drink, gamble, and socialize in whatever free time they had before they shipped out again.

For now, she was happy to let the others talk. All her attention was on the chubby child she held in her lap. Dana Armas had her mother's silver eyes and pale blue coloring, but there was something in the shape of her mouth and jaw that reminded Xori of the little girl's fathers.

The baby was fascinated by everything around her, from the cutlery on the table to Xori's hair. Currently, the child had a lock of it wrapped around her tiny fingers and was trying to pull it close enough she could put her hand and the hair into her mouth.

"Do you want me to take her?" Zura asked from across the table.

"What? Oh, no, she's fine." Xori freed her hair from the little female's fingers, trading it for a small piece of fruit. Dana crowed happily and crammed the morsel into her mouth.

"I don't know how you do it," Cynder had Dana's twin sister in her lap, bouncing the little one on her knee. "I have to admit, I was relieved when Alyson confirmed I wasn't carrying twins."

"Do you know if it's a boy or a girl?" Xori asked.

Cyn grinned. "We do, but we're not sharing just yet. You're new to the weird and wonderful ways of this crew, so you don't know about our tradition of betting on damned near anything interesting."

Zura laughed. "Odds are currently three-to-one that you're going to add another baby girl to the family. If you'd like to make a bet, I'm happy to take your money, Xori."

"I probably shouldn't." Xori said with a laugh.

"Why not?" Cynder asked.

"For the same reason I'm not," Chance said. "You've got a good idea already, don't you?"

Everyone stared at Chance, then at Xori.

"I haven't reached out, but I could. I'm not sure what I'd learn, since I sense emotion, not thought or form, but best I don't bet so no one thinks I'm cheating." Xori still hadn't gotten used to being open about her abilities. It wasn't common knowledge and never could be, but this group were her family now, and it had been freeing to let them in on her secret.

Cyn was quiet for a long moment, then handed Mya to the older woman sitting next to her. Phylomenia Harrington was a tall, lean woman with silver in her hair and lines in her face that deepened when she laughed, which was often.

"Hello, sprite," Phyl cooed to the baby, her eyes softening as Mya squealed with delight.

"Xori, could you? I mean, I'd like to know…" Cynder touched a hand to the subtle outward curve of her stomach.

Xori reached out and Cynder took her hand. Chance took Dana, leaving her free to focus on what she was about to do.

"This is a first. I don't know what I'll feel," she warned the cyborg female. Then she extended her awareness and focused it on Cynder.

In the week since bonding with her *vardo*, she'd been working on her abilities. For the first time she could actually practice *using* them instead of focusing on suppressing them. She sensed Cynder's emotions first. They were strong and clear as a mountain stream, with only a few darker patches where current worries and long-ago grief lingered. She moved past those and found something else. It was small and unfocused, but it was there, a life force so new it had no awareness yet.

She smiled at Cynder. "Your son or daughter is present, and as far as I can tell, they are content. I can't really tell you anything else."

Cyn smiled and squeezed her hand before letting go again. "That's good. Thank you."

Chance was taller than Xori, which meant Dana was

now high enough to be able to grab at the *matyri* Xori wore over one ear. It was a new design, one that had no relation to her social status. It was made of white gold, the metal twisted together at the center to form a star-shaped flower with sapphires for petals. It had been a mating gift from Vic and Ward, and she wore it with pride.

"Sha-sha," Dana burbled as she tugged at the ear cuff.

"Yes, it's very shiny, and it's not yours." Chance lifted the little girl away before she could get a good grip on the jewelery or Xori's hair.

Not that she would have minded. She loved spending time with the children, especially the way they reacted to Vic and Ward. They adored the two males, and the feeling was mutual. She suspected the twins were as much a part of her mates' recovery as anything she'd done. Unconditional love and trust were priceless gifts, and Zura's daughters gave both things freely.

"How are you feeling, Chance?" Nova Force had asked the uniquely gifted cyborg to review all the data to see what predictions she could make. The effort had drained her enough they hadn't seen Chance in two days.

"Better. I just wished there'd been more to go on. The Grays need to be stopped, but there wasn't enough data left on that ship to figure out where they were taking you, or what their next move might be."

Vivian might not have blown up the ship, but she'd destroyed it in every way that mattered. Nova Force had retrieved every object that had been expelled into space when the ship had vented atmosphere, including the bodies. They'd taken the Enigma 4 apart, but they hadn't found anything useful. The only clones on board were the two types she'd seen. There were no experiments in progress. The only DNA they'd found belonged to the clones or Xori, which confirmed that Vivian had never been present. All they had was the data she'd managed to take with her, and the knowledge that the Grays were watching their every move.

Security was elevated everywhere, especially with the big corporate event coming up fast. Tianna was determined to go through with it, pointing out that if she backed off now, it would only empower their enemy further.

"We don't know what the next move will be, but we can guess where it will happen," Zura said, her silver eyes clouded with worry.

"We'll be alright. We know what's coming and we're making plans. Taking care of each other. It's what we do here," Phyl smiled at Zura, then Cynder. "It's what you Armas folks have done since you started this place. Made it a home, a shelter against whatever storms may come."

Chance nodded. "One of the things I remember from my time on Haven were the storms. They'd roll in like every dark thing in the universe was coming for me. I hated them at first." She smiled, a little sheepishly. "Okay, I always hated the storms, which is why I live here now, but I did like one thing about them. After they passed, everything was fresh and new again."

There were nods and smiles from around the table and a general sense of comfort and support flowed between them. It was a nice feeling, made more so by the fact she was included in that comaraderie. She was part of the family now—the boundaries she'd created to keep her secrets were gone. She'd already endured one tempest, and it had reshaped her world. They would make it through this next one, too. And when it was over, she'd find a way to bring her parents to the Drift so they could see the life, and the males she'd chosen for herself.

Xori looked over to the gaming area, where her *vardo* were working. They were laughing and joking with the customers, but Vic caught her eye and smiled, holding up two fingers then pointing toward her. She grinned and nodded. They'd be going on break soon and she'd get to spend a few minutes with them before they finished up their shift while she went to the office to work. After they were all done for the day, they planned to wander the shops together looking for things to furnish their new rooms in the ever-growing family section of the club's staff quarters.

Cynder had joked that if their staff didn't stop falling in love soon, they'd have to expand the club, and Xori could see why. She had no idea how many beings lived within the relative safety and comfort of the Nova's walls until she'd become one of them.

Their new rooms were simple but comfortable, with space enough for the three of them to relax together.

They still had a lot to learn about each other, but she was happier than she could remember. She had a home and a family. One worth fighting for. She'd made her choice, and she'd stand with her mates to protect each other, and everyone who called this place home.

She finished her juice and pushed away from the table. "I'm going to spend a few minutes with my *vardo*, then I need to get back to work."

Zura groaned. "I need to get back to my office, too. I've got too many orders and not enough pilots."

Phylomenia raised a brow. "Who'd we lose?"

"Tucker and Banes. *Fraxxing* idiots were smuggling unlicensed pharma and thought I wouldn't find their hiding spot." She rolled her silver eyes. "Because no one would ever think to stash contraband in the gap between the inner and outer hulls of the cargo bay."

"Amateurs," Phyl scoffed.

"Exactly. If you're going to smuggle the good stuff, you've got to be smarter than that."

Vic and Ward were heading her way now, but Xori paused to ask. "So, you didn't fire them for doing something illegal? You fired them for getting caught?"

Zura nodded and grinned. "Yep. Welcome to doing business on the Drift, Dr. Virness."

Xori laughed and then said her goodbyes. She was only a few steps away when she heard Phylomenia cursing sharply.

"Son of a *fraxxing* starbeast. What's *he* doing here?" The older woman's normally relaxed drawl had deepened and taken on an edge sharp enough to draw blood.

It wasn't hard to figure out who 'he' was. Xori got a good look at the male as she walked slowly over to where Vic and Ward stood, just inside the VIP area.

The human male moved with a confidence that bordered on arrogance, his gaze scanning the crowd as if he were taking note of everyone and everything at once. His hair was black and marked by silver at his temples, and there was more silver in his close-cropped beard, but there was nothing about him that suggested infirmity, only experience. His clothes were tailored, dark and casual, but they might have been a uniform the way he wore them.

Thanks to her better-than-human hearing, she could still follow the conversation going on at the table she'd just left.

"Phyl, who is that?" Zura asked.

Phylomenia didn't answer the question. "Someone needs to contact Archer and let him know that when I'm done here, I'll be needing a word. You can also tell him that if he knew anything about this and didn't tell me, I will space his remains one piece at a time, starting at his feet and working up."

Phylomenia must have stood or done something to attract the male's attention, because Xori saw the moment he recognized her. For a split second, all his confidence vanished. He froze, staring. His lips moved, but he was too far away to hear what he said. The shock only lasted a moment, and then he turned and made his way toward them, a practiced smile replacing his surprise.

Vic gathered her into his arms and moved her to one side as Phylomenia stalked past them.

"Do we know what that's about?" He asked as he kissed her in greeting.

"No idea, but I think we should stay close in case she needs us."

Ward moved in behind her, pressing a kiss to the top of her head. "Hey, little star. We'll stick close, but if trouble starts, you let us handle it, okay? No going hellcat today."

"Alright." She winked. "Maybe tonight?"

Both males uttered a soft groan. "Yeah. Tonight's good." Vic said.

"And tomorrow," Ward added.

And forever. She cocked her head so she could hear what was being said between Phylomenia and the new arrival.

Even with the sound dampeners, she could make out every word. "Garrett Michaels. What the *fraxx* are you doing here?"

***

Thank You for Reading Dealers' Choice!

I hope you enjoyed Xori, Vic, and Ward's story.
If you're looking for more stories like this one, I invite you to explore the other books in the <u>Drift</u> universe, which include both the <u>Nova Force</u> and <u>Drift</u> series.

Susan lives out on the Canadian west coast surrounded by open water, dear family, and good friends. She's jumped out of perfectly good airplanes on purpose and accidentally swum with sharks on the Great Barrier Reef.

If the world ends, she plans to survive as the spunky, comedic sidekick to the heroes of the new world, because she's too damned short and out of shape to make it on her own for long.

You can find out more about Susan and her books at:
www.susanhayes.ca